First published in Great Britain 2022 by Farshore
An imprint of HarperCollins*Publishers*
1 London Bridge Street, London SE1 9GF

farshore.co.uk

HarperCollins*Publishers*
1st Floor, Watermarque Building, Ringsend Road
Dublin 4, Ireland

ISBN 978 0 7555 0388 9
Printed and bound in the UK using 100% renewable electricity at CPI Group (UK) Ltd

1

A CIP catalogue record for this title is available from the British Library.

LLAMA ON HOLIDAY

ILLUSTRATED BY
ALLEN FATIMAHARAN

ANNABELLE SAMI

Farshore

For Davinia who believed in this series,
and me, from the beginning. Thank you

CHAPTER ONE
Introductions

Everyone deserves a holiday. Lying on the beach, sipping an ice-cold fizzy drink, getting ridiculously hyper on ice lollies. We can all agree that summer hollibobs are the *best*. Even for secret agent toy llamas.

But I might have gotten ahead of myself there. If you don't know about Yasmin and Levi's secret agent adventures already, you won't know which stuffed toy llama I'm talking about. Well, I'll quickly fill you in: his name is Levi, he's a cockney toy llama and he can talk. A lot.

He's kind of like a fairy godmother to ten-year-old Yasmin Shah. Except not in a magical, turn-a-pumpkin-into-a-carriage way, more like a follow-you-round-and-annoy-you-to-death kind of way. He was sent to Yasmin to help her learn to stand up for herself and, with a lot of hard work from Yasmin, it worked! She got her parents to listen to her, she got to join art club instead of the science team and she gets better at communicating with people every day.

So a lot has changed since Yasmin found Levi in a pile of smelly socks at the bottom of her wardrobe. Since *she* actually ended up helping Levi keep his llama licence, Yasmin became an honorary guardian llama herself! (Just without the four legs and fluffy tail bit.) They've become quite the team, even if they do fall out from time to time (and trust me, even the best of friends fall out).

Speaking of friends, I can't forget to mention Ezra, Yasmin's best friend at school. Levi likes to take credit for getting them together, but it was actually checkers that formed their bond. They became such good friends that Yasmin even introduced him to the world of talking toy llamas

and the secret global llama organisation Seen Not
Herd.

It's a lot to take in, I know. It was a lot to explain.
To be honest, I think *I* deserve a holiday after all that.

But I want to tell you the story first. It's a good
one, and as you may have guessed, it takes place on
a sunny, seaside holiday.

Though nothing involving the Shah family and
a chaotic toy llama has *ever* been *that* relaxing.

CHAPTER TWO
Last Day of Term

The school bell rang to signal the end of lunchtime, but Yasmin ignored it. She hadn't completed her mission. It was the final day of school before half-term at Fish Lane Primary and the late May sunshine was getting everyone in a holiday mood. Just one more class before home time and the holidays could begin! But Yasmin wasn't rushing off to class just yet.

"Come on, come on, where are you?" Yasmin muttered under her breath, scanning the crowds in the playground for any sign of grubby llama feet. Where was Levi? Ezra would be here with Darren any minute!

Finally, she saw Levi, waiting behind a bin until all the schoolkids had cleared the playground to go back to class. Once the coast was clear he hopped out and made his way over to Yasmin, who quickly dropped to the floor and got into position. Levi ran over, singing his own James Bond style theme tune as he went.

"Dun, dun, *dun dun,* daaaa! Here I am, Yassy! And I got the goods –" Levi held up a sachet of ketchup that he'd taken from the cafeteria.

"Only one sachet?" Yasmin moaned. The ketchup was a vital part of the plan.

The head of the secret world organisation of guardian llamas (Seen Not Herd) was Mama Llama – a fabulous and no-nonsense lady llama. She was in charge of assigning Yasmin and Levi their missions, including their latest: helping a boy called Darren from the year below. After observing him for a few lunchtimes, Yasmin and Levi had quickly learned that Darren liked playing tricks on people. In fact, he was a bit of a bully. They'd tried to talk to him about it but he wouldn't listen to them. Not even when Levi revealed himself as a magic toy llama. One of Darren's favourite tricks was leaving particularly slippery and slimy banana peels by the swing set and waiting for people to trip on them. That's when Yasmin and Levi came up with their plan.

Yasmin heard the sound of her best friend Ezra's voice coming towards them from the boys' changing rooms out into the playground. He had been tasked with bringing Darren out at the right time.

"Quick, Levi, now!" Yasmin urged.

"Right, I'm on it!" Levi ripped open the ketchup sachet and squirted it all over Yasmin's face.

"Levi! It was supposed to be on my knee!" she cried. But then she heard Ezra and Darren approaching. "Never mind, here they come. Go hide!"

Yasmin started groaning as if she was in pain and Ezra ran up to her, ready to put on his best acting performance ever.

"Yasmin, what's wrong? You're bleeding!" he wailed, pointing at her face.

Darren gasped, eyes wide, and his hands flew to his mouth.

"I slipped on a banana peel someone left here and landed on my . . . face." Yasmin silently cursed Levi for putting the fake ketchup blood on her face rather than her knee like they'd planned. "It was *you* wasn't it!"

"I-I didn't mean it," Darren stammered. "It was just a joke. Oh no . . ."

Yasmin continued groaning for a while and Ezra even managed a fake sob before Levi jumped out from behind the swing set.

"Surprise!" he yelled, making Darren jump. "We got ya."

Darren looked at each of them in turn, his face confused. "You mean, you aren't actually hurt?"

Yasmin shook her head and wiped the ketchup from her face.

"So *you* tricked *me*?" Darren's cheeks went red. "And you got that stupid llama in on it too?"

"Doesn't feel so good being the one getting tricked, does it, mate?" Levi put his hands on his hips.

Yasmin stood up and put a hand on Darren's shoulder. "I'm sorry we tricked you. But we had to get you to see that the pranks you pull could hurt someone one day."

"Physically *and* hurt their feelings," Ezra added.

Darren sighed. "I never thought about that. I don't want to hurt anyone. I just wanted to be funny."

Yasmin nodded again and smiled. "Then maybe lay off the pranks and focus on telling jokes instead. Now you should get to class before you get into trouble."

Darren nodded in understanding and then ran off to his classroom. As they walked back in after him, Ezra spoke quietly to Yasmin.

"Another successful case for you and Levi. Mama Llama will be pleased."

"I hope so. It's sad that Darren will forget about Levi now we've finished his assignment though," Yasmin sighed. Once a child had been successfully helped by their llama guardian, they forgot about them, to help preserve Seen Not Herd's secret. It was a shame, but Yasmin knew it was necessary.

"I wouldn't have been able to do it without you, Ezra, my brilliant assistant."

"Um, *bodyguard*," Ezra corrected her.

"If you're Yasmin's bodyguard then can I be her boss?" Levi chipped in, head poking out of Yasmin's backpack.

"Phhst, not likely, either of you!" she replied, sticking her tongue out.

The three of them worked well as a team. Even if, technically, it was only Yasmin and Levi who were the guardian llamas, Ezra was Yasmin's voice when she didn't feel like speaking (and she did have her days). You see, up until a year ago, Yasmin used to not speak *at all*. It was only when Levi came along and convinced her that she deserved to be heard that she started talking. Even though she spoke now, she was still a quiet person. An introvert, as her elderly friend Gilly called her. She only spoke when she felt like it, which, compared to Levi, wasn't so often.

Yasmin liked being an introverted guardian llama and, if she did say so herself, they'd had a lot of success with their assignments.

Their first joint mission had been to help a girl in Year 1 make friends.

After some quick footie practice with Ezra, she felt confident to join in with lunchtime games.

Next, they helped Zeke with his science project presentation.

After some great advice from Levi, Zeke aced his presentation.

Just imagine everyone in their underwear.

They were there to support whoever needed it.

They'd completed every mission to date.

"Yasmin and Ezra." Miss Zainab put her hands on her hips. "Why are you five minutes late to my lesson?"

Yasmin felt her heart sink a little bit. "Sorry, Miss Zainab. We were helping someone in the year below."

"Sorry, Miss Zainab," Ezra echoed in a quiet voice.

Miss Zainab eyed them warily. "Hmmm, well okay then. Go to your seats. But I'm only letting it slide this time because I'm impressed with how well you've been helping other pupils this term."

Their teacher sat down at her desk and pulled out a huge stack of exercise books. Then she turned on the projector and Yasmin saw the opening scenes of *Squizz the Surfing Squirrel* on the whiteboard.

"Since it's the last lesson before the holidays you get to watch a film and do drawing," Miss Zainab said, picking up her red marking pen. "It's educational, of course, you're learning about . . . surfing and squirrels."

The class cheered! They'd also watched the first

hour of *Squizz the Surfing Squirrel* in their morning classes that day, but of course no one mentioned it. Yasmin peered down at Levi in her rucksack, who'd gotten out his glasses to watch the film.

"I love the last day of term!" he said, settling down to watch.

Once the film had started and the class were drawing and watching the film, Yasmin whispered to Ezra: "I got my acceptance letter to Riverbourne Academy this morning!" she said excitedly.

"Me too!" he whispered back. "Year 7 here we come."

Yasmin and Ezra fist-bumped each other. They'd planned to go to the same secondary school in September and Riverbourne had the best arts and music department in East London! Yasmin would be able to do art which she loved and Ezra could keep up his drum lessons – it was a win, win. Except . . . Yasmin looked down at Levi and bit her lip. He'd fallen asleep and was snoring loudly; not that any of their classmates could hear him. Although everyone could see him as a toy llama, Seen Not Herd agents like Levi could only be heard by the children they were helping.

"What are we going to do about L?" Yasmin whispered, making sure Levi was asleep. "I mean, it's one thing carrying around a weird toy llama here at primary school, where everyone already thinks I'm weird . . . but in Year 7?"

Ezra's expression darkened. "We'd be prime targets for teasing."

"For bullying more like." Yasmin frowned. "I don't want to upset L, he's told me he's excited to come to the new school with us. But I also don't want to be known as Weird Llama Girl."

"And I don't want to be Weird Llama Girl's Weird Friend." Ezra tapped his pencil on the table rhythmically. He always did this when he needed to focus.

Just then the little mobile phone that Levi carried

around buzzed in Yasmin's bag. Luckily, the sound of the film stopped anyone else from noticing. Levi snorted awake, eyes bleary and hair even more of a mess than usual. He flipped open the Llama Landline – a small silver flip phone that Mama Llama used to communicate with them.

"Yassy, you ain't gonna believe this," he perked up, jumping on to her lap under the table.

"What?" Yasmin was worried Levi had overheard their conversation somehow, but he seemed happy.

"I've just got a message from Mama Llama." He paused for dramatic effect. "We've been made agents of the month!"

Yasmin smiled wider than she had in ages. "That's amazing!"

Yasmin and Levi high-fived. Ezra cleared his throat.

"Sorry, mate. We couldn't have done it without ya!" Levi added, giving Ezra a high five too. "Imagine us three in Year 7. We're gonna be unstoppable."

Yasmin's smile faded and she shot a glance at
Ezra who also looked suitably awkward.

Brrrrriiiiinnngggg!

This time, everyone heard the high rattle of the
school bell. It was half-term! School was finished.

There was immediate activity as everyone packed away their pens and books, eager to get in line for pick up and the holiday to start.

"Half-terrrrmmmmmmmmm, let's do this!" Levi hopped off Yasmin's lap and back into her rucksack.

Yasmin sighed in relief. They didn't have to have *that* conversation. At least not yet.

The holidays had just begun!

CHAPTER THREE
Good News!

"What's for grub tonight then, Yassy?" Levi licked his lips as they walked through the front door after school.

"I dunno." Yasmin kicked off her shoes and looked around the kitchen. "Ammi isn't home from work yet, which means I've got time to do some drawing! Come on, let's go to my room."

Levi's stomach rumbled. "But Yassy . . . I'm starving!"

Yasmin gave him a chocolate digestive (one of his top three fave biscuits). Then she popped him on her shoulder and headed up to her room. This was no easy task since she lived on the fifth floor of an extremely tall, thin house. She had to go through every single one of her large and loud family's rooms before she got to hers in the attic.

First up was her twin aunties, her papa's sisters, who lived in the room above the kitchen.

"There she is!" Auntie Gigi pinched Yasmin's cheeks and gave her a big red lipstick kiss on her forehead. "How was the last day of school, flower?"

Yasmin thought about it . . . A lot had happened at school that day. But she simply smiled and said, "Okay."

Even though she was getting better at it, making conversation still wasn't Yasmin's favourite thing to do.

"It's so cute how you still carry around that toy I got you for your birthday last year," Auntie Bibi gushed, pointing at Levi on Yasmin's shoulder. "I'm the best at choosing presents."

"I am a pretty great present," Levi bragged. Yasmin stifled a giggle, since only she could hear Levi's jokes.

But Auntie Gigi frowned. "I don't know, sister, don't you think she's getting a bit too old for cuddly toys? She's going to secondary school in September."

Yasmin's stomach tightened in embarrassment.

"Nonsense, sister. She can still have cuddly toys!" Auntie Bibi retorted. "I had a teddy bear until I was thirty-three and I turned out *just fine*."

"Speak for yourself," Auntie Gigi said, looking her sister up and down.

Yasmin left them arguing and hurried up the stairs. Her aunties had a unique way of holding a conversation about you as if you weren't standing right in front of them.

"I ain't a cuddly toy! I've been working out," Levi complained as they headed up the stairs and through her parents' room. Both her ammi and papa weren't home yet so she estimated she had at least half an hour of drawing time before they got back.

"Look, check out my biceps. Pow!" Levi held out a

single skinny, fluffy leg.

"Mmm, *very* strong," Yasmin joked, poking it.

She reached the door of the next floor up – her brothers' room – took a deep breath and held it. (The deep breath was necessary to brace herself but also for the stench.)

"Well, if it isn't Trombone," Tall Brother announced, sitting playing on his phone in bed. Yasmin's brothers had given her the horrible nickname of Trombone after hearing her unusually low voice for the first time.

"We heard you're coming to our school for secondary," Short brother snorted. "You better not embarrass us!"

Yasmin rolled her eyes and walked through their room quickly, still holding her breath.

Levi blew a raspberry at her brothers on her shoulder. "Tell 'em the only thing that's embarrassing is their haircuts."

Yasmin let go of her breath, giggling. Her brothers

had both opted to get 'cool' haircuts recently, which involved Tall Brother getting the underside of his hair shaved and Short Brother getting blond highlights. The barber had *not* done a good job.

But Yasmin kept her mouth shut and walked up to her room. She'd learned that communicating didn't just mean talking – it meant knowing when to speak. Even though teasing her brothers might feel good in the short-term, she knew it would come back to bite her in the bum in the future.

Yasmin's attic bedroom was her own personal paradise. It was quite small and the walls sloped down from the centre to the edges like a tent, so she had to bend down to sit at her desk. But it had everything she loved in it. Posters of the universe and historical maps on the walls, plus her pride and joy – a massive chalkboard on the wall behind her bed. It was made from a special kind of paint that turns any surface into a chalkboard. Papa had painted it on her wall for her seventh birthday after they realised how good she was at art. Yasmin used it to doodle and hatch plans on, using her sketching pad for more detailed work. She'd drawn her most amazing daydreams of being a secret agent in the sketch pad – long before she actually *became* one in the form of a human guardian llama.

After changing into an oversized hoodie and shorts, Yasmin spent a solid half hour drawing whilst Levi snoozed on her bed. Before long she heard Ammi and

Papa arrive home from work downstairs and start cooking together. It wasn't difficult to hear them since her parents were possibly the loudest people to ever walk the face of the earth, *especially* Ammi who only spoke in shouts and all at the same time. After a while the familiar call came up the five flights of stairs and reverberated around the house.

"KHANATAYAARHAI. COMEANDEAT!"

But this time it was followed by something else.

"WEHAVEEXCITINGNEWS."

Yasmin and Levi immediately looked at each other, eyebrows raised. (Yes, Levi had eyebrows, you just had to look *really closely.)*

News? Yasmin was intrigued.

"Put me in your pocket, I wanna hear this for meself." Levi jumped at Yasmin from the bed and she caught him, stuffing him in her hoodie pocket. Already smelling the delicious aroma of dinner wafting up the stairs, Yasmin headed to the kitchen where everyone was already sitting down to eat.

Ammi had made keema and okra which Yasmin loved, and luckily so did Levi. Despite being made of stuffing and fluff, Levi seemed to be able to eat food, though Yasmin wasn't sure where it all went ... Frankly, she didn't want to know. When everyone started tucking in, she spooned Levi little bits of her dinner under the table.

"So what's this news then, sister?" Auntie Gigi pressed.

"Yes, don't keep us waiting." Auntie Bibi's eyes shone. Both aunties were not patient, especially when there could be a hot piece of gossip or news to discuss.

Ammi and Papa shared a look, which Yasmin couldn't read. Something was up for sure. Finally Papa cleared his throat.

"Well, sisters, the good news is we're going on holiday!" He sat upright and smiled.

Everyone around the table made excited 'Oooooooohhh' sounds, but Yasmin knew that wasn't the whole story. Papa looked at Yasmin and her brothers.

"We will be going to visit your ammi's sister who has just moved to Whitehove," Papa said brightly.

"ITISABEAUTIFULSEASIDETOWN," Ammi said proudly, dishing food on to her plate.

"Cool!" her brothers said in unison.

"Not in a million years!" Auntie Gigi clattered down her knife and fork.

"After what your sister did to us!" Auntie Bibi was

suitably shocked.

Levi's ears pricked up. "Here we go, what's the drama?"

Yasmin sighed. She *knew* the drama all too well. Auntie Bibi and Gigi had long accused Ammi's sister, Auntie Rani, of stealing their prized biryani recipe. It was the biggest family scandal of 2011.

"Bibi and Gigi, as your older brother, I am telling

you to end this ridiculous feud," Papa said in a booming voice, though Yasmin noticed his moustache twitching nervously. "Rani is a good woman and I'm sure she didn't steal your recipe."

"How else did she know to add a teaspoon of tamarind and sugar then?" Auntie Gigi's voice was sharp. "Thievery!"

Ammi sighed and Papa put his fingers to his temples.

"So, sisters, you *won't* be joining us on holiday?" Papa groaned.

"Certainly not," Auntie Bibi answered for both of them.

Yasmin knew that trying to change her aunties' minds was like trying to dig a hole to Australia with a teaspoon – impossible and exhausting. But then a different thought popped into Yasmin's mind. In the past she would have been afraid to ask her parents for something, since they almost always said no. But with Levi sitting in her lap, she felt confident.

"Ammi, Papa . . . if the aunties aren't coming, then there will be a space in the car, right?" Yasmin asked.

"Yes, why?" Papa replied, recovering his composure.

"Well, I was wondering if Ezra could come with us instead?" Yasmin ploughed on. "Tall Brother and Short Brother just hang out with each other all the time anyway, so it would be nice if I had someone to play with."

"Um, not fair!" Tall Brother shouted. "And stop calling us those names!"

Ammi held up a hand to get silence. "FINEBUT WE'LLASKEZRA'SPARENTSFIRST."

Yasmin and Levi secretly high-fived under the table.

"Nice one, Yassy," Levi congratulated her.

"But you have to include your cousin Omar when you're playing." Papa wagged a finger at Yasmin.

"Of course, baby cousin Omar is cute!" Yasmin

agreed. It had been a couple of years since she'd seen her cousin but she remembered him as a chubby-cheeked little kid with big brown eyes. He could tag along with her and Ezra just fine.

Yasmin ate the rest of her dinner feeling very pleased with herself. Not only might she be going on holiday with her best friends, but she'd actually asked her parents for something ... and *got it*. The old Yasmin would never have done that.

Later on, when Yasmin and Levi had gone up to her room to watch TV after dinner, Ammi called up the stairs again.

"YASMINEZRAISONTHEPHONE."

"Thanks, Ammi!" Yasmin called back down using the megaphone she'd bought for this very purpose.

She ran to the phone in her room but Levi got there first, picking it up with both of his skinny arms.

"Allo, allo," he said into the headset. "You comin' on hollibobs with us then?"

Levi tapped the speakerphone option and Yasmin

heard Ezra's voice on the other line.

"We're all going on a summer holidayyyy!" Ezra sang. Yasmin and Levi cheered.

"Yes, this is gonna be sick." Levi clapped his feet together. "A group holiday before we head into Year 7. I gotta pack!"

Yasmin's stomach tightened again. Levi really wanted to come to Year 7 with them ... She grabbed the phone as Levi headed over to the cupboard and started digging through his small number of belongings. Toy llamas don't really have to wear clothes, but Levi liked to have a few pieces for added 'swag'.

"Hello?" Yasmin put the receiver to her ear.

"Yas, am I off speakerphone?" Ezra asked quietly.

"Yep."

"When are we gonna tell him about Year 7? I feel bad, but he can't come with us ..." Ezra trailed off.

Yasmin sat down heavily on the bed.

"After the holiday, I promise," she whispered.

Ezra sighed. "Okay. I trust you. See you on Sunday."

Yasmin hung up the phone and forced a smile at Levi who had poked his head out of the cupboard.

"Everything all right love?" He cocked his head to one side.

"Yep!" Yasmin forced a big smile at him. "We're off on holiday!"

A whole week without any secret agent guardian llama business and, most importantly, no school.

This was gonna be fun, right?

CHAPTER FOUR
We're All Going on a ...

"I spy with my little eye something beginning with ... A! No. T ... No, wait, S!"

Ezra's face was glued to the window of their seven-seater people carrier as Ammi raced up the motorway, hands gripping the wheel. Ezra had started this game of I Spy with Yasmin what felt like a hundred hours ago, but he could never settle on a word for Yasmin to guess!

It was a hot day that really put the 'sun' in Sunday, so Papa was blasting the air-conditioning. They'd left London early, to 'beat the traffic' as Ammi liked to say, but they'd already got stuck in several traffic jams. Yasmin kept having to remind herself she was on holiday. The fun was just beginning! Just as soon as they got out of this car ... Yasmin's phone pinged and she looked down to see a text message from her friend Gilly. They'd met when Yasmin was volunteering at the elderly people's day centre on Brick Lane and stayed friends ever since. Gilly might have been in her late eighties but she texted like a twelve-year-old.

Gilly: U on holz yet?
Yasmin: On the way. Be back in a week.
Gilly: Kk. Game of checkerz when ur back?
Yasmin: For sure. See you then!
Gilly: C u l8r.

Yasmin put her phone away and scanned the view from her window for anything starting with S. She was rudely interrupted by her brothers kicking her seat from behind.

"Punch Buggy blue!" Tall Brother yelled out, punching Short Brother in the arm.

"Punch Mini red!" Short Brother yelled back, whacking Tall Brother in return.

They'd made up a ridiculous game where spotting certain cars meant you got to hit the other person in the arm. Yasmin didn't ask to play but she was, unfortunately, dragged into it.

"Stop. Them. Kicking," Levi spluttered out, lying weakly across Yasmin's lap. Levi got carsick. Bad. Or at least, he really milked it if he was feeling ill. He sighed dramatically from time to time, requiring Yasmin to rub his back or give him sips from her apple juice carton.

Yasmin was just about to guess 'seat' when Ammi swerved dramatically into the slow lane and everyone in the car screamed.

"WATCHWHEREYOU'REGOINGIDIOT!" Ammi bellowed, shaking her fist at the car in front who had cut them off.

A road trip might have been fun if Ammi didn't have road rage. In fact, Yasmin would go so far as to call it road *fury*. But as the only designated driver in their family, they had no choice but to let her loose behind the wheel.

Papa broke the terrified silence by joining in with his favourite song that had just come on Desi Gold Radio, singing his heart out in the entirely wrong key. He didn't seem too bothered that they had just narrowly avoided death.

Yasmin took a deep breath and let it out slowly. This was a lot. And there was still another hour left of the journey!

"Ezra, I think I'm done with I Spy now. Sorry." She stroked Levi's clammy back. "We need to get as much peace as we can in this car of chaos."

Ezra nodded. "No worries, I've brought my GameHype console anyway."

Levi groaned again and motioned for a sip of juice, which Yasmin gave him, wondering how much of this was put on for show.

"Look at Yasmin pretending to give her stuffed

toy a drink!" Tall Brother jeered, peering at her from the back seat.

"She's such a baby," Short Brother joined in.

Yasmin quickly put the juice down and felt her cheeks blush. To everyone else Levi just looked like a regular stuffed toy and that made Yasmin look like a baby, apparently.

"Ugh, I can't believe we have to go to the same secondary school as *them*." Levi flung a dramatic arm over his eyes. "I can't take it!"

Ezra immediately whipped his head round to stare at Yasmin and opened his mouth to speak, but she widened her eyes and mouthed, *Don't Say Anything Yet!*

"LEAVEYOURSISTERALONE," Ammi yelled over her shoulder, still gripping the wheel and hunched forward like a Formula One racer, despite being well within the speed limit.

The brothers complied and settled back in their seats. No one argued with Ammi, especially when she was in full Hulk mode behind the wheel.

The next ten minutes were filled with the sounds of Desi Gold Radio, Ezra's video game and her brothers' arguing, but Levi managed to fall asleep which Yasmin was grateful for. Every time he mentioned Year 7, she felt even guiltier about not wanting him to come. It was blowing up like an uncomfortable balloon in her stomach and she was worried at any moment it would pop in a huge guilt explosion. But if her own brothers, who saw him every day, thought Levi was embarrassing, then what would the other kids at Riverbourne Academy think?

(Side note, but I imagine a guilt explosion to look like green gloop and smell like boiled cabbages.

Or just something very, very smelly.)

Yasmin looked out of the window at the stretching motorway and closed her eyes. Only one hour until sea, sunshine and ice cream . . .

"WE'REHERE."

Yasmin bolted awake. It felt like she'd only just closed her eyes but apparently a whole hour had passed by! Her neck was stiff from sleeping at a weird angle and she was mortified to realise she'd been dribbling. Hopefully nobody had noticed . . .

"All right Yassy." Levi yawned and stretched on her lap. "You could be a pro basketball player with all that dribbling."

Of course *Levi* had noticed.

"Look, Yasmin, is that your family?" Ezra pointed out of the window and Levi bounced over on to his lap to peer out too.

They were in a small close of houses, all detached, red brick, and much bigger than Yasmin's. They all had freshly mown front gardens and pretty flower beds. It seemed like the sun was shining just to make the picture even more perfect! Standing in the doorway of the house they'd pulled up to were three figures.

"Auntie Rani!" Yasmin beamed, happy to see her auntie smiling and waving at her. It had been so long since her auntie had last visited them in London and Yasmin had fond memories of her.

Auntie Rani was standing, glamorous in a sequinned shalwar kameez and gold bangles on her wrists. Next to her was Uncle Yusef, in a smart white shirt and loose linen trousers. His thick black hair was oiled and gleaming and he beamed at the car.

Ammi was straight out of the driver's seat, running

to her younger sister with open arms.

"Um, is *that* the 'cute little cousin' you were on about?" Levi asked this time, gazing in the direction of the driveway.

Yasmin turned to the driveway and couldn't believe her eyes. Her sweet baby cousin Omar *definitely* wasn't a baby any more. He was taller, wearing Nike Air Forces with spiked-up hair and he was overturning plant pots in the driveway to poke at the ants underneath.

Yasmin, Ezra and Levi stumbled out of the car, stretching their cramped legs from the long journey. Auntie Rani saw Yasmin and brightened, though her face twitched. It was only now that she was closer that Yasmin realised her smile seemed forced.

"Omar, come say hello to your cousin and her friend," Auntie Rani called over to her son.

What happened next explained Auntie Rani's twitching.

Omar straightened up and at the top of his lungs screamed,

"NO!!! I HATE YOU!!!!!!"

Then turned and ran into the house, leaving a stunned and awkward silence behind him.

"Wow . . ." Levi huffed. "I knew we should'a got a hotel."

CHAPTER FIVE
... Summer
Holiday

Auntie Rani and Uncle Yusef helped carry in all the luggage, which consisted of:

1. A huge leather suitcase the size and weight of a double-decker bus. This was Ammi and Papa's shared suitcase and they always took it on holidays. It had been around since before Yasmin was born and could probably withstand a nuclear bomb.

2. Three shopping bags filled with containers of food that Ammi had cooked. Yasmin had no idea why she did this since Auntie Rani had already prepared them plenty of food. But Yasmin knew her mum wouldn't be caught dead arriving at a

relative's house without at least a tub of chicken pilau (and maybe some vegetable curry on the side).

3. A smaller (though still large) suitcase full of gifts for Auntie Rani to take back to Pakistan for various family members, as she was visiting next. The gifts ranged from chocolate shortbread biscuits all the way up to a power drill.

4. One small duffel bag each for Yasmin, Ezra and the brothers since, in Ammi's words, 'THERE'SNOROOMINTHEBOOT.'

They hauled everything inside, before sitting down at the table to eat some lunch. It had been a long drive and Yasmin was hungry, so the masses of delicious plates of food in front of her were a welcome sight.

"Oi, get me one of those fishcakes, Yassy," Levi called from her lap, reaching his leg out to see if he could pinch one before anyone saw. But Yasmin

quickly slapped his foot away. No one else had started eating yet, as Auntie Rani was trying to coax Omar down from his room. She stood at the bottom of the stairs, still forcing that strained smile and calling in a bright voice.

"Omaaaaaarr, come and eat, darling. Everyone's here and they want to say hello."

"I don't," Levi mumbled.

There was a loud stomping and Omar appeared at the landing, his round face screwed up in anger. Omar was nine, a little bit younger than Yasmin and Ezra, but his baby face made him appear younger. If he wasn't frowning so much then Yasmin thought he would still look cute.

"I *don't want to*," he sulked, folding his arms across his chest. "And I'm *not* having *them* stay in my room."

When he said this he was glaring, eyes narrowed, at Yasmin and Ezra. Yasmin gulped. It seemed they were all going to be room buddies this week. Ezra cleared his throat and Yasmin instantly knew that whatever he was going to say would *not* go down well with Omar.

"It'll be fun, Omar, like a sleepover or something." Ezra grinned at the stroppy boy at the top of the stairs.

"Sleepovers are for BABIES!" Omar fumed, and ran off back to his room.

Tall Brother and Short Brother sniggered

amongst themselves and kicked Yasmin under the table. She secretly hoped that wherever her brothers were sleeping was damp and smelly.

Auntie Rani sighed heavily and came to join the family at the table, Uncle Yusef putting a supportive hand on her shoulder.

"I'm so sorry, everyone, I just don't know what's happened to our sweet boy." Auntie Rani looked at Ammi, who shook her head sadly. "As soon as we moved here it's like his personality changed overnight."

"ITCOULDBEAPHASE," Ammi suggested, tucking into the food. "YASMINDIDTHESAME."

Yasmin scoffed. *As if.* She was the best-behaved child ever!

"We hope so," Uncle Yusef agreed. "We've tried speaking to him about it but he doesn't want to talk to us."

"We pray to Allah for some magic or a miracle that Omar will return to his usual self." Auntie Rani looked upwards as if she was asking heaven directly.

But Papa tutted through a mouthful of chapatti. "There's no use waiting for a miracle, Rani Bhabi. What Omar needs is good old-fashioned discipline! Everyone knows magic isn't real."

Yasmin caught Ezra's eye and they suppressed a smile. The magical talking toy llama on her lap would suggest otherwise. Nevertheless, she agreed that something definitely needed to change with Omar, otherwise this holiday might not be as fun as she'd expected. Auntie Rani said his behaviour had changed as soon as they moved here from Pakistan . . . that must have something to do with it . . . *No!* She stopped her thoughts and started piling her plate up with food. This was supposed to be her holiday. No more guardian llama business!

After eating a massive lunch, the family spent the rest of the day hanging out at the house. Auntie Rani was a doctor and Uncle Yusef ran a business from their home. He had his own office and everything! When they settled down to watch a Bollywood film in the evening Omar slunk into the room and watched with them, picking at leftovers on the table. Yasmin tried talking to him a few times but he simply scowled at her and turned the other way. Ezra didn't seem too bothered by Omar's sulkiness though. He was *completely* engrossed in the colour and music of the Bollywood film despite not being able to understand a single word.

"I've gotta say, those Bollywood peeps know how to make a film," Levi said in Yasmin's lap, munching on some popcorn. "It's got more drama than an episode of *EastEnders*!"

Eventually it was time to go to bed, and once again Omar was putting up a fuss. His bedroom was big enough to put out two single mattresses for Yasmin and Ezra on the floor. Yet he was running around his room, flailing his arms and claiming that the beds 'took up all the space'.

Yasmin sighed and reminded herself that her

brothers were having to share a small, pull-out bed in the office, which brought her a bit of comfort. At least she and Ezra had space. Plus, Omar seemed to have all the latest toys and a flatscreen TV in his room! As soon as the adults had gone and they'd got ready for bed, Omar turned to Yasmin and Ezra.

"DON'T touch any of my stuff. You can't use the TV and you *definitely* can't use my games consoles."

"Well, that's not a good way to make friends,"

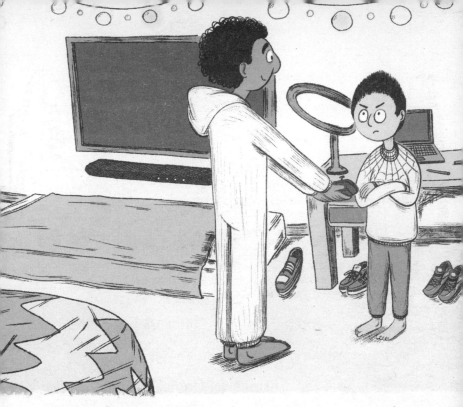

Ezra exclaimed. "Look, here's my games console. You can use it if you want."

Ezra got his GameHype console out and Omar's eyes widened slightly. But then he caught himself and got into bed, turning over to face the wall.

"I don't want to play with you. Yasmin's pyjamas make her look like a *baby* anyway."

Ezra shrugged and put the console down on the side but Yasmin went bright red. She looked down at her pyjama shorts and top. They were unicorn print and multicoloured. Were unicorns babyish? She just thought the print was cool. But Levi, who had settled himself on her camp bed, saw her burning cheeks and piped up.

"I think they're *really* cool, Yas," he said. "Funky,"

Yasmin groaned. "Thanks. But that somehow makes it even worse."

"Who are you talking to?" Omar snapped over his shoulder, making Ezra and Yasmin jump.

"Oh, no one," Yasmin said quickly, jumping into bed. "No one at all."

This was going to be an interesting holiday.

CHAPTER SIX
A New Mission

"I told you I *don't like* choco-wheats!"

Omar banged his fists on the table, making the cups and plates rattle.

"Watch it, Omar," Tall Brother warned, holding his mug of chai steady.

Yasmin and Ezra rolled their eyes at each other. It had been like this ever since they'd woken up that morning. Omar had got up on the wrong side of the bed, except by all accounts, it was an everyday occurrence. But Yasmin was still determined to have a good time. This was the first day of their half-term holiday and the excitement of beach frolics and ice cream was enough to make Omar's bad mood bearable.

They were having breakfast in Auntie Rani's big, open-plan kitchen, all sitting down at a large round table. Ammi was cooking parathas and fried eggs for the adults over the stove but Yasmin had specially packed her favourite breakfast cereal 'Bear Bites'.

Levi was tucked inside her dressing-gown pocket, yawning loudly and munching on bits of fried egg that Yasmin swiped for him. It was like having a permanently hungry gremlin in her pocket, but she was so used to it now that she kind of liked it. It would seem weird not to hear Levi calling up at her from one of her pockets. Like when she went to Year 7 . . . Yasmin shook her head.

None of those thoughts, please, she told herself.

"Auntie Rani," she asked quietly. "Where did you put my Bear Bites cereal please?"

"In the tall cupboard over there, sweetheart," her auntie replied. "Such a polite girl!"

"Can I have another egg, please, Mrs Shah?" Ezra called to Ammi, scraping the remnants of his plate into his mouth.

Ammi laughed and plopped the egg on to Ezra's plate, patting his head. Yasmin knew her ammi had a soft spot for her friend. Anyone who loved her cooking went straight in Ammi's good books.

When Omar saw Yasmin filling her bowl with her special cereal he started laughing and pointing. "You know that cereal is supposed to be for *little kids*, right? Look at the packet! There's cartoons on it."

"But I am a kid." Yasmin was confused. All kids liked Bear Bites didn't they? They tasted like honey *and* they were shaped like bears. What was not to like?

"You're supposed to be older than me." Omar folded his arms and smirked. "Even I don't eat baby food."

Yasmin's brothers burst out laughing. Short Brother even snorted out the orange juice he was glugging down, through his nose!

"Omar, that's enough!" Uncle Yusef said firmly, immediately silencing the table.

Yasmin looked down at her cereal, feeling a bit embarrassed. Should she be eating more grown-up cereal since she was nearly at secondary school? What even was grown-up cereal – a bowl of raisins and prunes? Black coffee instead of milk? Gilly always had porridge topped with M&Ms for breakfast, but she wasn't like a normal old person anyway.

"Chin up, love." Levi patted Yasmin on the leg. "Don't let him get in ya head. We're on holiday, remember."

"Yay, holiday!" Ezra cheered, following Levi's lead

and getting some weird looks from the table.

Yasmin smiled and dug into her bowl of Bear Bites. *I'm on holiday!* she thought. *Nothing's going to get me down.*

>BEEP BEEP BEEP<

A high, electronic beeping prompted the adults at the table to check their phones. But Yasmin knew from the vibration in her fluffy grey dressing-gown pocket that it was the llama landline. Was it a new message?

"Excuse me, I need the loo," Yasmin said, hurriedly getting down from the table and running to the bathroom.

"She looks desperate," Tall Brother said loudly. "Hope those Bear Bites aren't coming back to *bite* you in the bum."

Yasmin heard giggles but she ignored her brother and headed into the bathroom, locking the door behind her.

Levi emerged from her pocket, laughing and wiping his eyes. "Sorry, love, but that was quite funny."

Yasmin snatched the llama landline from Levi's grasp and looked at the message. From the small icon picture of a sandy-coloured llama with red lipstick and pointed-tip glasses, Yasmin knew immediately the message was from Mama Llama:

Message received at 10.05am

From: Mama Llama

To: Agent Levi and Agent Yasmin

Subject: NEW MISSION

YOU HAVE BEEN ASSIGNED A NEW MISSION BY MAMA LLAMA

MISSION DETAILS: HELP OMAR

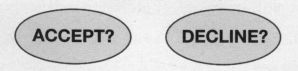

Yasmin stared at the screen for a while, blinking rapidly. She tried scrolling down the page but there was nothing there.

"That can't be it? No more details?" she murmured to herself.

"What? What is it?" Levi scrambled up from her pocket on to her shoulder.

"'Help Omar', that's all it says! Help him with what? Not being really annoying?" Yasmin exhaled heavily and sat down on the bathroom floor.

Levi studied the screen himself, holding it up *very* close to his eyes since he wasn't wearing his glasses.

"A new mission, huh . . . and here I was thinking we'd get a holiday." Levi shook his head in frustration. "Still. Omar *does* need help."

Yasmin looked at Levi dubiously. *Surely* he didn't think they should actually take the mission?

"Think about it, Yassy." Levi could read her looks pretty well by now. "The only way we're actually gonna enjoy this holiday is if we get Omar to stop acting like he's got a bee in his bonnet. Plus, don't you wanna help your family?"

Levi stared at Yasmin with his beady eyes, silently trying to convince her to take the mission. (It got weird after a while since he didn't need to blink.) It made sense that Levi wanted to accept – helping kids was his whole reason for existing! But Yasmin was a guardian llama now too and that came with responsibilities . . . After thinking it through, she relented.

"Ugh! Well we are 'agents of the month', it wouldn't look good if we declined the mission."

Levi cheered, hopping up and down. Then there was a soft knock on the door.

"Yas? It's Ezra. You okay? How's your stomach?"

Yasmin opened the door and quickly pulled Ezra in. "My stomach's fine! My brothers were winding me up."

"Phew. So what's the actual emergency?"

Yasmin showed Ezra the screen of the llama

landline and gave him a minute to read it.

"Are you going to take it?" Ezra said, looking to Levi and Yasmin in turn.

"Even though he's so rude to me . . ." Yasmin began.

"And this is supposed to be our holiday . . ." Levi joined in, standing on the closed lid of the loo.

"We're gonna do it." Yasmin held her hand out and Levi fist-bumped it.

"Great!" Ezra joined in the fist bump, making it a weird triangle fist bump.

"On one condition!" Yasmin said suddenly, remembering Omar's taunts over the past morning and night. "I don't think we should tell him about Levi."

Levi dramatically dropped to his knees. "What? Why? Surprising the kids is my favourite bit!"

"Mine too." Ezra did a dramatic pout. "It's like giving someone a present."

Yasmin stood her ground. "Omar has already made fun of my pyjamas and my cereal for being too babyish. What do you think he'll say if he knows I have a magical, stinky, dirty toy llama too? He'll just make fun of me!"

"Hey! That's not nice!" Levi protested.

The guilt balloon in Yasmin's stomach inflated a little bit. But she wasn't giving in on this.

"I'm sorry, Levi. But that's my condition."

Levi and Ezra looked at each other, making up their minds.

"I'm here to help you, Yasmin." Ezra smiled. "As your bodyguard."

"Assistant." Yasmin winked back. "Levi?"

Levi was shuffling his feet and looking down at the ground, "All right. I'm in. But you gotta stay open to revealing me *if* we need to."

"Deal!"

Yasmin opened the llama landline and pressed the ACCEPT button.

"Okay, Omar. Prepare to be helped."

CHAPTER SEVEN
All the Fun
of the Fair

Funfairs should be *fun* right? I mean the word is right there in the name. So you would think that every kid would be over the moon to visit a funfair *on the beach*. Well, Yasmin, Ezra and her brothers were excited. But Omar . . . well, you'd think Omar was being dragged to go underwear shopping. He *did not* want to go.

After breakfast, Yasmin had changed into her striped summer dress (the only dress she'd ever be caught wearing) and packed Levi into her beach bag. He'd somehow found a pair of sunglasses small enough to fit his tiny head and had even insisted on Yasmin putting sunscreen on his nose, despite her telling him cotton didn't burn.

Then as a huge group, the family tramped down to the seaside, which was only fifteen minutes from Auntie Rani's house. Uncle Yusef had to drag Omar by the arm the whole way down.

"I don't want to go, I want to stay home and play my video games!" Omar shouted.

"Don't be ridiculous," Uncle Yusef said through gritted teeth. "Your cousins are here and we are all going to have a *nice time.*"

Yasmin and Ezra caught each other's eye. Uncle Yusef said 'nice time' with the anger of someone who was definitely *not* having a nice time. They hung back a bit and let the group walk ahead of them.

"Okay, so plan of action," Yasmin began, pulling Levi up to the top of her bag so he could hear.

"Blimey, it's baking hot in there," Levi said, adjusting his shades and peering out.

"I think to help Omar, we first need to understand what's wrong." Yasmin was proud of her plan of action. She'd been thinking about it all morning. "How would you describe his attitude at the moment?"

"Angry, moody, irritable," Ezra listed, counting on his fingers.

"Annoying, pain in the bum," Levi chimed in.

"Says *you*," Yasmin pointed out, narrowing her eyes at Levi.

"Fair point." Levi thought for a moment, bouncing up and down in Yasmin's bag as she walked. "He seems . . . sad."

Yasmin nodded. "He started acting like this when he first moved here, so there must be something about this place that he doesn't like." She looked out at the sparkling sea in the near distance as they approached the seafront. The sky was clear and the sun was shining – who couldn't like this place?

Yasmin continued explaining her plan.

"I think we should try and get him to lighten up at the funfair. Actually have some . . . you know, fun.

There's no way he's going to open up to us at the moment. But maybe once he's enjoying himself, he might start to talk to us more. I'm calling this: Mission Fun-in-the-Sun Fair."

They'd reached the seaside now and the family group was waiting for them up ahead. There was a paved promenade all along the edge of the sandy beach lined with deckchairs and brightly coloured beach houses. To the right of them in the near distance was a large pier that stretched out into the sea. There seemed to be a big, tall building on it, lit up with neon lights and signs.

But the thing that really got Yasmin's holiday brain excited was the funfair stretched out in front of them, right on the beach! There were little stalls set up on the sand with various games and fast food stands dotted around. A big red and white helter skelter towered above them on the left, and there was not one, but THREE roller coasters.

"Yeah, yeah, the plan sounds great, Yasmin," Ezra

mumbled, looking up at the largest roller coaster in awe.

"I need a large candyfloss and a go on the bumper cars IMMEDIATELY." Levi clapped his front feet together.

Yasmin collected her thoughts. "Okay, focus, everyone. We're on a mission, remember? Luckily . . . the mission is to have fun. Specifically, to get Omar to have fun."

She looked over at her younger cousin, who was

sullenly standing between his mum and dad with a face like thunder. This might be harder than she thought.

They joined everyone and the adults gave them some rules for the funfair.

(What, you didn't think they'd just let the kids run riot did you? This was Ammi and Papa we were talking about!)

"YOUCANGOONFOURRIDESEACH," Ammi instructed, handing out the tokens they'd bought at the ticket booth.

"We will wait here, come back in one hour exactly," Papa said, wagging his finger.

Then the parents sat down at a bench in the shade of one of the food stalls, already exhausted from the heat. Ammi was wearing her lightest long-sleeve dress in sky blue and a matching headscarf. Papa had weirdly chosen jeans and a smart shirt for the beach, insisting that 'summer in England is nothing compared to Pakistan!' though Yasmin saw large sweat patches forming at his armpits.

Tall Brother and Short Brother immediately ran off into the fair, leaving Ezra, Yasmin, Omar and Levi (hidden in Yasmin's beach bag) to roam the fair.

"Whoop, this is gonna be fun, Omar," Yasmin said enthusiastically to her cousin. "What do you want to go on first?"

He blinked back at her and then with a straight face commented, "Your voice is really weird. It's low."

"Yeah, people call her Trombone," Levi giggled.

"Who said that?" Omar whizzed his head round, looking for the source of the sound. Yasmin whacked her bag against her side, giving Levi the sign to shut it. Now that they were officially his guardian llamas, Omar could hear Levi too! Yasmin chewed her lip. She hadn't considered this when she made Ezra and Levi promise not to reveal him. Getting Levi to shut up when Omar was around was going to be hard.

"How about the helter-skelter?" Yasmin tried again, forcing a smile.

"*How about the helter-skelter?*" Omar mimicked, making his voice low.

Yasmin huffed and walked ahead, trying to keep her cool.

"That wasn't nice . . ." she heard Ezra say to Omar behind her. Trying to help someone who was so rude was a huge challenge.

Yasmin spotted her brothers up ahead at the water pistol shoot-out booth, ready to play a round. *Perfect,* Yasmin thought, *a bit of friendly competition to get things started.* She stormed off towards the booth, with Ezra trying to keep up behind her.

"Wait, we're joining this round too!" she bellowed at her brothers, making the boy running the stall jump a little.

"Suit yourself," Tall Brother announced. "Get ready to be annihilated."

Ezra and Yasmin picked up their water pistols, aiming them at the paper circles they needed to break through with the water stream. But Omar just leaned heavily against the wall of the booth, kicking the sand with his foot.

"Come on, Omar, let's play," Ezra encouraged.

"No way! This game looks stupid."

"Pistols at the ready, players," the boy conducting the booth instructed. "In three, two, one . . ."

Yasmin was surprisingly good at water pistols and broke through three of her targets in a row. After her laser tag shoot-out victory a few months ago though, she should have expected to be good.

"Remind me never to get on your bad side," Levi whispered, peeping out of the beach bag. "You have scarily good aim."

The bell rang and Yasmin roared in celebration. She'd won! Her heart pumped and she realised that the annoyance she'd felt for Omar might have turned into competitiveness. Tall Brother and Short Brother threw the pistols down in frustration.

"Fine, hook-a-duck next, I bet you won't beat us at that," Tall Brother taunted, heading over to that stall.

"I bet I will!" Yasmin retorted, immediately following her brothers.

"Wait, Yasmin. Remember the *plan*," Ezra said under his breath, chasing after her.

But Yasmin wasn't listening. She'd got whipped up by her brothers' teasing and could think of nothing better than channelling that frustration into a game of over-competitive hook-a-duck.

It was only when she'd aggressively hooked her second rubber duck that Ezra finally got her attention.

"Okay, Yasmin, you've had your fun, now what about Omar?" he said, turning around to where he expected Omar to be. "He was . . . he was right behind me, wasn't he?"

Yasmin's ears pricked up and she dropped her hook. "What did you say?"

"I don't know where Omar is," Ezra said, frantically scanning the crowds. "He's gone!"

"Blimmin' heck, this is a disaster!" Levi popped his head out of the bag. "See, this is what happens when you don't let me keep an eye on things!"

"Everyone, shh." Yasmin looked out over the crowds of the fair. "Let's just find him before the parents or Mama Llama realise we lost him."

"Cool, have fun with that. We're gonna go on the helter-skelter." Tall Brother grinned, collecting his prize for hooking the golden duck.

Yasmin whirled around to locate the helter-skelter – and suddenly she saw Omar, standing in line at the top of the slide. "There he is!"

"Well, what are you waiting for?" Levi scrambled out of the bag, hopped up on to Yasmin's shoulder and pointed straight ahead. "Let's go, go, go!"

Too late! Omar is off again.

"Come on, Omar," Yasmin said, jumping out of her car. "We only wanted to hang out with you today and all you've done is run away."

Ezra jumped out of his car too and both of them walked over to Omar, who was staying put this time. Yasmin put a hand on his shoulder but he shrugged it off.

"What's wrong, Omar? Don't you want to have fun?" she asked gently.

"Funfairs are stupid and childish. Let's just go back to our parents," Omar grumbled, though Yasmin noticed he was looking over her shoulder. She turned around and saw some kids about Omar's age getting into the bumper cars for the next round. Omar jumped out of his car and walked off ahead.

"But the fun's only just started," Levi moaned, getting back into his hiding place in Yasmin's bag. "I wanted to see how many times I could smash the car into the side before they ask us to leave."

"I know but we have to do what Omar wants. We're helping *him*." Yasmin followed her cousin. "And I don't think your legs are long enough to reach the pedals anyway."

They tracked Omar back to where the adults were sitting in the shade. Ammi was fanning herself with a flip-flop and Auntie Rani had several empty iced-coffee cups in front of her.

"Oh, thank goodness you're back, we're melting out here," her auntie said, quickly jumping up.

"Where are your brothers?" Papa asked, looking around.

Ammi lifted her head up and yelled,

"TARIQ!!!!!!!!!!!!!!!!!!!!!!!! HAMZA!!!!!!!!!!!!!!!!!!!!!!!!!!!"

It was so loud that everyone on the beach stopped what they were doing and turned to stare at them. Yasmin was surprised that the seagulls didn't drop out of the sky.

Tall Brother and Short Brother came running towards them, both carrying crazy amounts of blue candyfloss. When they got closer Yasmin noticed their eyes were wide and both their tongues were bright blue.

"How much sugar have you had?" Yasmin screwed her nose up. Not even she could eat that many sweets!

"Dunnoprobablyabouttwobagseach," Tall Brother said, extremely fast and all in one go.

"I don't feel very well," Short Brother said, looking a bit pale and clutching his stomach.

"Okay, time to go." Uncle Yusef clapped his hands together. "I think we've all been in the sun too much. Did you have fun, Omar?"

Omar stuck his tongue out at his dad and stomped off ahead.

Yasmin sighed. So much for getting Omar to open up after a fun day at the fair.

"I had fun!" came Levi's muffled voice from inside Yasmin's bag.

Mission Fun-in-the-Sun Fair was a flop.

CHAPTER EIGHT
Behold! A Guardian Llama

As soon as they got back, Omar was punished for sticking his tongue out at his dad.

Uncle Yusef was taking Papa's advice about Omar 'needing discipline' and sent Omar to his room for the rest of the evening.

"Oh no, not my room where all my toys are!" Omar said sarcastically as he stomped upstairs. "I'd rather hang out in my room than with *them*."

Once again, that hate filled *them* was directed at Yasmin and Ezra. They needed a team discussion. Yasmin led Ezra to Uncle Yusef's office, which was luckily empty. She brought Levi out of her bag, placing him on the desk.

"Okay, new plan needed." She looked from Ezra

to Levi, her face expectant.

"You know what I'm gonna say, love." Levi cocked his head to one side. "Introduce me!"

Yasmin blew her cheeks out and made a *phhhhsttt* noise.

"I have to agree with Levi," Ezra said, using some pencils as makeshift drumsticks. "We can tell him you're here to help and be his guardian llamas. Be honest."

"And you can't have guardian llamas without the *Llama*." Levi struck a jaunty pose.

Yasmin wrung her hands. She understood their point, she really did, but she was still worried about revealing Levi.

"What if he makes fun of me for having a talking toy llama as my best friend?" She chewed her lip.

But Levi waved his arms around.

"Um, hello? That's cool! Besides, you're gonna have to introduce me to all your new mates in Year 7 anyway. Obviously, they won't know I'm magic but they'll still wanna know my name."

Yasmin stayed absolutely silent. She could feel Ezra's eyes on her like lasers, but she avoided catching his glare. They weren't telling Levi until *after* the holiday.

"Kids, dinner's ready!" Auntie Rani sang up the stairs.

"KHANATAYAARHAI!" Ammi screamed after her, just in case someone hadn't heard the first time.

Yasmin nodded slowly. "Okay. You're right. We do need to reveal Levi to Omar. Maybe if we explain we're here to help and that Levi's like a weird fairy godmother, he'll realise we're serious about helping him. Let's do it after dinner."

Ezra beamed and put his hand out, followed by Levi who put his furry foot on top. Yasmin smiled and placed her hand on top as well, feeling good to be supported by her two best friends.

They all threw their hands up and cheered in unison, "TEAM LLAMA!"

Dinner was a delicious spread of Mexican food that Uncle Yusef prepared, having travelled for business to Cancun last year. Yasmin didn't know exactly what her uncle did (something to do with computers?), but it sounded fun being able to travel around for work. Maybe she'd start a business when she was older if it meant she got to eat Mexican food as part of it. Being a guardian llama seemed to come with world-travelling opportunities too, but as far as she could tell, Levi wasn't getting paid for his services.

After they were stuffed full of cheese, rice, plantain and chicken, Yasmin gave Ezra a 'look' that meant the reveal was about to happen. They waited until they were allowed to get down from the table and Omar ran to his room straight away.

"I guess we'll do it in Omar's room then," Yasmin whispered, and beckoned Ezra to follow her. Levi had stayed in the bedroom while they were having dinner so Yasmin swiped him an empanada before dashing upstairs.

She took a deep breath before knocking softly on the door and opening it a crack. Omar was playing on his games console in bed, whilst Levi stood motionless on Yasmin's mattress. He was eerily good at pretending to just be a stuffed animal, but then again, that was the point. It was a disguise . . . though not for much longer.

"Why bother knocking if you're just going to come in anyway?" Omar muttered, not lifting his eyes off his game.

"Ha, yeah, good point." Yasmin stood awkwardly next to his bed. Her stomach was churning and she realised she was really nervous. She hadn't been this scared to reveal Levi to the other kids she'd helped, so why Omar? Her mind flashed back to the nasty remarks her younger cousin had made about her being babyish . . . Levi was definite bullying material – that was why she didn't want to take him into Year 7. What if Omar confirmed those fears?

"So, Omar, we were wondering if we could talk to you about something?" Ezra stepped in, making Yasmin relax. She knew what she wanted to say, but not being a big talker, it was a massive help to have Ezra there to be her mouthpiece.

"About what?" Omar spat.

"We wanted to know if you're happy here," Ezra said, sitting down on Omar's bed. Yasmin joined him, trying to keep her face neutral so she wouldn't scare Omar off. Her cousin paused his game and peered up at them.

"What do you mean?" he frowned.

"Well . . . Yasmin and I noticed you seem kinda unhappy. We were wondering if it's something you don't like about living here in this new place," Ezra went on. "If you let us know what's wrong, we could help you!"

Yasmin could see Omar shrinking away from

them, moving further towards the top of his bed, pulling his knees up to his chest. She knew that he was feeling scared. They were going to lose him.

"Listen, Omar," she jumped in. "We do really want to help you. In fact, it's kind of our job. You see . . ."

Yasmin walked over to her mattress and picked Levi up. The llama was still motionless, though he did wink at her. She popped him down on the bed in front of Omar.

"Me and this . . . llama. We're guardians. We help kids who need a bit of support. Levi was my guardian llama and now we do it together." Yasmin stopped and took a deep breath, feeling her cheeks burn. Omar was looking at her like she'd just admitted to being a hula-dancing racoon, which frankly wasn't that far off in terms of weirdness.

Omar spoke slowly. "So you're telling me that you and this . . . *toy*, are here to be my *guardians*?"

"Yes." Yasmin bit her lip. "And he's magic."

Ezra grinned. "Ta-da!"

Omar blinked at them in disbelief.

"Levi . . . now would be a good time to, uh, you know. Be magic." Yasmin nudged the llama.

Levi stayed completely still.

"Levi!" Yasmin nudged him again. "Sorry, he's kind of *really annoying*. Stop playing around."

Omar was looking from Ezra to Yasmin with wide eyes. He slowly started inching towards the door.

"LEVI!" Yasmin finally boomed in her low voice.

Levi jumped up into the air, did a somersault and landed in the splits.

"Behold!" he yelled. "It is I, Levi the guardian llama!"

Yasmin put her face in her hands.

"All right, all right. I don't actually talk like that." Levi walked up to Omar and held a leg out. "I'm Levi and yeah, like Yassy said, we're here to help so, uh, what seems to be the problem?"

Omar stared at Levi's outstretched leg for a while, his mouth open. Then, he suddenly grabbed

Levi and turned him upside down.

"Whoa, whoa, what are you doing?" Levi complained.

"Looking for the switch so I can turn this thing off," Omar grumbled, searching Levi's matted fur.

"I'm real! This is one hundred per cent, mate," Levi huffed, wriggling out of Omar's grip and running over to Yasmin for protection.

Omar switched his console off and put it away in the drawer next to his bed. "Yeah, right, my friend back in Karachi has a robot dog that speaks thirty languages. Whatever you paid for that, you got ripped off."

"But . . . but, Levi is really magic. And we're *really* here to help you," Yasmin pleaded.

"He's not real. You're just trying to trick me." Omar walked over to the door. "I know all about making fun of people. I'm going to watch TV with my parents."

Before they could stop him, Omar walked out of the bedroom, slamming the door behind him. As it banged shut, Yasmin felt all the hope inside her fizzle away. Usually, revealing Levi was the best part of the mission – it got the child they were helping to really take the guardian stuff seriously. But for Omar it had done the exact opposite.

"Well . . . try again tomorrow?" Levi chirped.

"Ugh, this is a disaster!" Yasmin flopped back on the bed. "We're never going to complete this mission. He's a lost cause. And *so mean.*"

Levi jumped up on to her belly, almost winding her.

"Come on, love, we can't give up at the first hurdle. He's not a lost cause. I've had way more difficult kids."

Yasmin lifted her head to stare at Levi. "Really?"

Levi waggled his eyebrows and grinned.

"You mean me!" Yasmin chucked a pillow at him and both he and Ezra laughed.

"You threw me in a rubbish truck! You buried me in the garden! You even dobbed me in with Mama Llama. But I never gave up because I was your guardian llama." Levi poked her in the belly.

"Levi's right." Ezra joined in with the poking. "There's more going on with Omar, we just need to get him to trust us. That won't happen overnight."

Yasmin nodded and something Omar said

replayed itself in her mind – '*I know all about making fun of people.*' What had he meant by that? There was definitely more to uncover. She pulled herself up out of bed and clapped her hands together.

"You're right. I'm not going to give up at the first hurdle. Thanks, guys, you're the best." She smiled at Levi and Ezra. "Oh, and Levi, I swiped you this."

She threw the beef empanada at Levi and he caught it in his mouth, biting into it and getting sauce all down his grey fur. Yasmin and Ezra giggled as he tried to lick it off.

"Blimmin' heck, that's gonna stain. I gotta wash this off." Levi hopped off the bed and stopped by the bedroom door. "And Yassy? Don't worry, you're still just learning how to do the guardian llama stuff. Look at me – it took me a while. But we're a team. I'm always gonna have your back, girl."

He trotted off into the bathroom, shutting the door behind him.

Remember that guilt balloon in Yasmin's stomach?

Yeah, it was about to burst.

"UGH, I feel awful." She hid her face with the cushion. "Maybe we should just let him come to Year 7 with us."

Ezra laid down on the bed next to her and sighed. "I feel bad too. But we know what the other kids will say – especially the older ones. We can't keep him hidden all day in a locker either – I'm pretty sure that's animal cruelty, even if the animal is a toy."

"He's just so keen on coming everywhere with me," Yasmin said quietly. "And I like it, I just . . . I want to have a fresh start at secondary school. Where no one thinks of me as the weird quiet girl who walks around with a stuffed llama. Omar's right – it is childish."

"I love Levi too, but I don't want to be bullied," Ezra said seriously, drumming his hands on his lap. "Carrying around a toy is really going to make us stand out to everyone else."

"So we'll still tell him he can't come to Year 7 *after* the holiday?" Yasmin looked over at Ezra and held her little finger out.

"Deal," Ezra agreed, wrapping his little finger around hers.

Yasmin groaned and held her guilt-filled tummy.

It wasn't going to be easy to keep holding in the truth but at least Levi could still enjoy his holiday. Not telling him was the kindest thing to do.

At least, that's what Yasmin thought.

CHAPTER NINE
Oh I Do Like to Be Beside the Seaside

A summer holiday wouldn't be quite the same without a trip to the beach. But there are a few rules in beach manners we need to get straight before continuing this chapter. These are *very serious* rules, so pay attention!

DO NOT FEED THE SEAGULLS. Especially not chips. Even if you feed just one seagull, in a millisecond an entire army of those flying terrors will be dive bombing your chippy dinner. And let's not even mention the threat of plops from above . . .

TAKE YOUR RUBBISH HOME WITH YOU!

You can wee in the sea . . . but save anything else for later. I mean, this one should be obvious, right!??

Now that's out of the way, let's go forth into this

chapter. As you've probably guessed, it takes place at the seaside and absolutely none of the above rules get broken. Not once.

Ezra was tossing chips up into the air and letting seagulls catch them in their beaks as the adults set up their beach chairs.

"Ezra, sweetie, don't do that. They won't leave us alone," Auntie Rani said kindly.

"EZRASTOPIT," Ammi yelled, struggling to unfold her chair.

Ezra immediately shoved the last of the chips into his mouth, sneaking one to Levi who was in the pocket of his beach shorts.

"Blimmin' scavengers," Levi tutted at the seagulls as they flew away. "Give us another one, Ezra."

Uncle Yusef and Papa hammered a large umbrella into the sand and opened it up, casting a nice cool shadow on the ground beneath. It was a very hot day for May, which is why Auntie Rani had suggested the beach, and Ammi was already sweating through her kaftan. She and Auntie Rani collapsed into their beach chairs under the umbrella and Yasmin could tell that they wouldn't move from those positions for the rest of the day.

Tall Brother and Short Brother immediately tore off their T-shirts and let Papa slap some sunscreen on them before running head first into the sea. Yasmin watched them dive under and start splashing water at each other. It looked fun, but Yasmin was a little nervous. She'd only been to the sea once before, and since she couldn't swim, always stayed in the surf.

Ezra must have noticed her looking nervous and reached out to squeeze her hand.

"It's okay, Yasmin, I'll stay with you in the shallows," he smiled.

"And I'll be staying right *here*," Levi said curtly. "Put me down on your towel, Ezra. I ain't going nowhere near the water. Saltwater makes my stuffing itch."

Ezra obliged and laid Levi down on his beach towel. Levi didn't seem to be enjoying the beach, but Yasmin figured he was just afraid of the water like her. He immediately got out the llama landline and started tapping away on it.

Yasmin heard huffing and turned around to see Omar, crouched behind his mum's beach chair and fiddling about in the sand. Time to try again.

"Hi, Omar. Do you want to come and make sandcastles with me and Ezra?" she asked, trying to make her voice peppy.

"*Nope.* I'm not five," he replied, not even looking up.

"Omar, don't be rude," his mum scolded.

Yasmin shrugged. Like Ezra said, he wouldn't trust them overnight. She'd just have to keep trying.

The water was cool and inviting even in the shallows. Yasmin and Ezra lay down on their bellies and had lots of fun, pretending to be fish, flopping about and getting splashed when the waves came in. Yasmin even used her art skills to draw pictures of her and Ezra in the sand with a stick. Then they collected their buckets and started making sandcastles with the wet sand.

"I'm going to make Bucketham Palace," Yasmin winked, tipping her bucket upside down and patting the bottom. "It's going to be . . . regal."

"I'm making a sand drum kit!" Ezra enthused,

shaping sand into cylinders around him. "I just need to find some drumsticks . . ."

Further out in the sea Yasmin heard her brothers laughing and saw Tall Brother spike a beach ball at Short Brother's head. Then Short Brother grabbed the ball and did the same back to Tall Brother. She rolled her eyes. They were so childish sometimes!

"Hey."

Yasmin turned her head to see Omar standing above her, blocking the sun with a big bodyboard he was holding.

"Hey, Omar, did you come to play with us?" Ezra smiled up at him.

"No. I don't want to play stupid sandcastles. But you should come bodyboarding with me in the sea," Omar said quietly.

Yasmin beamed. This was a good step! Omar wanted to include them. There was just one problem . . .

"I can't go out there with you. I can't swim," she explained. "But –"

"Ugh, whatever!" Omar was immediately furious. "If you don't want to come bodyboarding with me then just say it, don't make up an excuse. You're just like everyone else!"

Omar raised his foot and in one swift kick, completely flattened Bucketham Palace!

Yasmin gritted her teeth and dug her hands into the sand to stop herself shouting at him. He was such a brat! But she was his guardian llama ... She looked over to where Levi was sitting, typing on his phone still. Who was he messaging? He should be helping with the mission!

"Hi, Omar!" came a voice from behind Ezra.

It was a boy, around Omar's age, with light brown hair, a button nose and freckles. He seemed sweet. And he knew Omar ...

But Omar simply looked at the boy and scowled, before running into the sea and diving in.

"Well, that's one way of avoiding people ..." Ezra mused.

Yasmin caught the brown-haired boy's eye. "Hi, I'm Yasmin, Omar's cousin. How do you know him?"

The boy looked down nervously. "From school. I'm Jack."

"I'm Ezra! So are you friends with Omar then?"

Jack shook his head. "Not really. Omar doesn't

have any friends at school. I've tried to talk to him but he always seems angry. I've seen him hanging out with some other kids at lunchtime though."

Yasmin and Ezra looked at each other with raised eyebrows. Now *this* was interesting. This could be a lead in finding out why Omar didn't like it here in Whitehove.

"What are those kids' names?" Yasmin asked.

"Jason, Harrison and Hannah." Jack frowned a little when he said their names. "I'm not friends with them, but I see them talking to Omar a lot."

Yasmin got up and brushed the sand from her hands. "Thanks, Jack, you've been really helpful."

Jack smiled and gave them a small wave before running off back to his parents.

Ezra looked up at Yasmin, shielding his eyes from the sun.

"What are you thinking?" he said. "I know that look on your face."

Yasmin held out her hand and pulled him up.

"I think there's something that Omar doesn't want to tell us." She looked over again at Levi, lying on the beach towel and looking every bit like an inanimate toy llama at the beach.

"Come on, it's time to share our findings with the llama."

Levi might not want to get involved with the sea, but he had to get involved with the mission. They were a team after all.

CHAPTER TEN
Party Planning

"Levi, Levi! We've finally got something to go on."

Yasmin ran over to her beach towel, kicking sand up as her feet hit the ground. She suddenly became aware of Auntie Rani and Uncle Yusef looking at her suspiciously. Ammi and Papa were used to Yasmin talking to her stuffed toy llama, and thought it was just one of her quirks. But with the adults around, Yasmin and Ezra wouldn't be able to discuss their plans openly.

"Shall we go build sandcastles over there?" Yasmin said to Ezra, pointing to an empty spot on the beach away from prying eyes or ears.

"Yeah, sure, I can work on my drum kit again!" Ezra said, racing ahead. Yasmin followed behind, quickly picking up Levi as she went.

As soon as they'd got far enough away, Levi jumped out of Yasmin's hands and on to the sand.

"Can I help you?" he said curtly.

Yasmin blinked in surprise. "What's up with you? I thought you'd be happy. Whilst you were playing with your phone, we found something out about Omar which can help the mission."

"So we're not actually building sandcastles?" Ezra seemed a little disappointed.

Levi's tail whipped from side to side in annoyance. "I wasn't 'playing on my phone'. I was doing well important work stuff . . ."

Yasmin raised her eyebrows, unconvinced.

"Anyway, what did you find out?" Levi's ears had perked up, so Yasmin knew he was interested.

She told Levi about how Omar didn't have any friends at school and how the other boy, Jack, seemed keen to talk to Omar.

"Oh, that's easy then." Levi hopped up and down,

suddenly seeming much happier. "We just need to help him make friends. I'm great at that – I got Ezra to be mates with you."

Yasmin put her hands on her hips. "Um, you didn't 'make' him, he liked hanging out with me!"

Ezra chuckled. "So what's the plan then? I became friends with Yasmin because we both liked checkers. We don't know anything Omar likes doing. Only what he *doesn't* like doing."

Levi was already pacing back and forth on the sand, thinking. Then he stopped and lifted his front leg. "I've got it! We'll have a beach party here tomorrow. We'll invite the kids from Omar's school and plan games that Omar likes to do. At least one of the kids has got to like the same things as him, right?"

Yasmin nodded along as she listened. "This could really work. But we have to prepare first. Ezra, you're good at talking to people. Can you be in charge of the guest list? Try and invite everyone from Omar's class."

"Got it!" Ezra saluted Yasmin and ran off in the direction of Jack.

"Levi, you're obviously on fun and games. You can organise the activities."

Levi smiled and puffed his chest out. "I am *really* fun. But wait, we still don't know what Omar likes to do."

Yasmin narrowed her eyes and searched out Omar, who was splashing about in the shallows by himself.

"Leave that to me."

After safely placing a very sandy Levi back on her beach towel, Yasmin slowly walked towards Omar on the shoreline. She felt like she was approaching a wild animal that would run off if she made any sudden movements. She would never admit it, but her heart was beating a bit faster having to talk to Omar. Even though he was younger than her he made Yasmin a little nervous. But she was his guardian llama, and the thought that Mama Llama trusted Yasmin to look after him gave her the confidence she needed to go forward.

"Hi, Omar."

Her cousin turned around and immediately started to get up from his place in the surf.

"No, wait. I was just wondering if I could ask you something." Yasmin waited until Omar seemed to be staying put.

"Go on then." Omar pouted, whooshing his hands around in the water.

"I was wondering what you like doing for fun?"

Yasmin asked gently. "Like, what do you play with the kids at school?"

"Everyone at this school is boring," Omar replied immediately, frowning.

"Okay, well, what did you play with your friends at your old school?"

Omar thought for a while and Yasmin noticed his scowl soften. "I liked volleyball. Me and my friends would play tournaments at lunchtime. We had this game called Pogo cards as well. I had the best collection! You played against each other and traded cards."

Yasmin noticed that this was the most Omar had spoken to her. *He must find it easier to talk about his life back in Pakistan,* she thought.

"That sounds fun." Yasmin smiled. "It must've been really rubbish having to leave all your friends. Is there nothing you like about living in Whitehove?"

The crease between Omar's eyebrows appeared again. "I like the sea I guess. I like bodyboarding a lot. Anyway, I'm gonna get an ice cream."

And in a flash, Omar had got up and left. Yasmin realised he'd probably reached his limit for sharing that day. But that was okay, she'd found out what she needed. Omar liked volleyball, bodyboarding and something called Pogo cards.

All she needed to do now was ask the adults to let them come back to the beach again tomorrow and come up with a cool name for the beach party plan. Her possible options at the moment were:

The (Beach) Ball Plan?

Mission Fin-possible?

Operation Shell-ebrate?

Ah, never mind. Levi would probably come up with a better name anyway. Either way – the mission to help Omar seemed closer than ever to completion.

Bring on the party!

CHAPTER ELEVEN
Fun, Sun and Sudden Death Volleyball

The final name that Levi settled on for the super amazing beach party hangout they'd planned the next day was:

Levi's Sun-believable Beach Party

Yasmin had argued that it was a bit wordy to be a code name for an operation but Ezra's suggestion of 'Sandy Beach Get Together Thing' wasn't much of an improvement.

(If you have any better suggestions, reader, please do let me know.)

But the name of the plan didn't matter, it was the *execution* of it that counted, and Yasmin was certain they'd got everything worked out. Jack had assured Ezra that he would invite everyone in their class.

There would be no adults around as Ammi had made Tall Brother and Short Brother come along to be their 'chaperones' (annoying but better than parents) and Levi had planned out some fun activities for the group to play. Of course, they couldn't tell everyone that a talking toy llama was leading the party games, so Ezra was going to act as Levi's spokesman.

Even though Auntie Rani had forced Omar to come, Yasmin felt quietly confident that their plan was going to work. As they walked down the road that led to the seafront, they spotted Jack waiting by the only pink beach hut, which they'd agreed would be their meeting point.

"Uhhhh, where's all the kids?" Ezra said, scanning the beach.

Yasmin's heart dropped. Standing next to Jack were only three other children – two boys and one girl. But she held her chin high.

"We'll make it work," she said quietly, then to the

group, "Look, there's that boy from your class, Omar, let's hang out over there."

Omar suddenly stopped in his tracks. "I don't want to hang out with them."

Ezra moved closer to him and linked his arm. "It's okay. We'll all be together. Plus, look, they've brought bodyboards."

Omar sighed heavily, but with nowhere else to go, he trudged along beside Ezra. Yasmin caught Ezra's eye and her best friend mouthed to her, *he's shy.*

But Yasmin wasn't so sure. He had only stopped walking when he saw the other kids. Maybe it was just them he didn't like? But they'd already planned everything out and come this far. It would be a shame not to go ahead with the Sun-believable Beach Party now.

"We're gonna sit over there away from you lot, don't do anything weird," Tall Brother said, leading them on to the sand.

"Yeah, Ammi said you're our responsibility so

don't get us in trouble!" Short Brother agreed.

They walked over to the group and laid out their towels, with Tall Brother and Short Brother setting up their area a far enough distance away that they wouldn't be associated with the 'kids'.

"Hey, I'm Harrison," one of the new kids said, stepping forward. He had jet-black hair that fell over one eye in a fringe.

"I'm Jason." Another boy stepped in line with Harrison. He was quite short and had red hair and freckles.

"I'm Hannah," the tall girl said last. "Who are you?"

Yasmin was a little taken aback. The kids seemed quite direct, more so than she ever was at their age. But then again, at their age, Yasmin didn't even speak.

"I'm Ezra and this is Yasmin. Yasmin is Omar's cousin. You guys know him from school, right?"

The children nodded silently in response.

Yasmin shifted uneasily on the spot. So far the

party was a little awkward. More like a parents' evening than a beach hangout.

"Right, time for some games I reckon," Levi announced, making Omar jump. "Bodyboarding competition, who can ride a wave the longest?"

Ezra relayed the message to the group and everyone grabbed a board. As they headed to the water, Yasmin noticed Omar looking over his shoulder at Levi in her bag. *Maybe he's finally realising that Levi is magic,* she thought.

As the afternoon progressed and the party went on, Yasmin actually started to feel like she was on holiday.

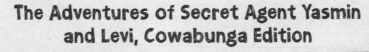

The Adventures of Secret Agent Yasmin and Levi, Cowabunga Edition

The winner is Omar, who rode a wave for ten seconds!

Volleyball tournament!

TEAM ONE

TEAM TWO

That's a foul!

That's a foul too!

Yasmin starts to suspect something's up . . .

Omar was getting more and more infuriated – as anyone would if a volleyball was being repeatedly spiked at your head. This wasn't good. The whole point of getting activities that Omar enjoyed was to help him make friends, but at this rate he was going to give up. The opposing team kept saying 'oops' or 'my bad' when they hit Omar, but Yasmin suspected they were doing it on purpose. Maybe Omar wasn't friends with Harrison, Hannah and Jason for a reason . . .

But before Yasmin could call off the game and share her suspicions with Levi and Ezra, she saw them conferring with each other.

"This game is getting a bit boring," Yasmin heard Levi say to Ezra. "Time to liven things up. Look in that bag."

Levi had made Ezra lug a huge bag of 'party props' to the beach with them, and Yasmin saw Levi whisper something into Ezra's ear whilst pointing at the bag.

"Um, Ezra!" Yasmin called, trying to get his attention and continue the game at the same time.

But Ezra wasn't listening. He looked a bit unsure, but following Levi's instructions, he cupped his hands around his mouth and bellowed,

"SUDDEN DEATH ROUND!"

Yasmin and Omar caught each other's eye . . . this couldn't turn out well for them.

In one swoosh, Ezra picked up the bag and emptied six inflatable volleyballs on to the court. Yasmin just saw the gleam in Harrison's eye as he and his teammates ran for the balls and started raining inflatable fury on them from above!

"Retreat!" Yasmin yelled to Omar and Jack as they avoided getting hit.

"We win!" Jason laughed, poking his tongue out over the net.

Omar stomped heavily in the sand. "This was a stupid idea. I'm not playing any more. They're picking on me."

He ran off to the beach towels and lay face down, Jack following him.

Yasmin turned to catch Levi's eye. He was propped up on a beach chair, looking awkward. She narrowed her eyes at him.

"What part of the plan included a 'sudden death' round, hmm?" she hissed, pacing over to him.

Levi shrugged. "I thought it would liven things up . . . Oops."

Yeah, you could say that again.

CHAPTER TWELVE
The Balloon Bursts

"The clue is in the name, Levi," Yasmin whispered angrily. "Sudden DEATH. Does DEATH sound fun to you?"

Ezra slapped his hand to his forehead. "I knew I shouldn't have listened to you, Levi. Now Omar's upset again. And we just started having fun together."

Levi took his sunglasses off and looked Yasmin in the eye. "I know that sudden death thing might have been a bad idea . . . But don't worry, I've got something planned for the final activity that's going to blow your socks off."

"You'd better be right." Yasmin whispered, trying not to raise suspicions. "Because I don't think

Harrison, Jason and Hannah are too friendly. Maybe we should just call the party off."

"No! Just one more activity. Trust me," Levi said. "They're gonna play with those Pogo cards. I found them in Omar's room. How bad can an innocent Pogo card be? They're in that bag of party supplies."

Yasmin sighed. She had to trust him, they were partners. She opened up the party supply bag and saw a blue folder inside. Confused, she picked it up and opened it, surprised to see it full of shiny trading cards.

"Those are Pogo cards, huh?" Ezra looked at the folder over Yasmin's shoulder. "I think I recognise them."

Each card had a different strange fantasy animal on it, with various abilities listed below. Omar had organised them into little plastic pockets, neatly displaying

them in colour-coded pages.
Yasmin smiled, thinking of her cousin
taking pride in his collection.

"Okay, Levi. I hope this works."

She stole a glance at Omar, who was
angrily digging in the sand, though he was letting
Jack join him. Jason, Harrison and Hannah were
sitting in a group a little way off, whispering and
sniggering together. Yasmin felt a
big ball of doubt forming in her
mind. Were these really kids that
Omar wanted to be friends with?
Just because Jack had seen them
talking a lot at break times didn't
mean they were trying to be friends
with him. But Levi seemed convinced, as
did Ezra, and Yasmin was worried that
she might be letting her feelings about Omar's
rudeness get in the way. So she gripped the folder
tightly in one hand and Levi in the other, slipped

The Dark Lord
Mittens
Strength 10
Speed 10
Cunning 1
Wit

her flip-flops on and strode in between the two groups.

Once Omar caught a glimpse of what Yasmin was holding, his eyes widened, his cheeks went bright red and he instinctively reached for the folder. But Yasmin was so determined to make *everyone have fun* that she didn't even notice. She had Pogo tunnel vision.

"Hi, everyone. Next fun activity," Yasmin called, holding the folder aloft.

"As chosen by yours truly," Levi added, causing Omar to glare at him furiously.

"We're going to play with Omar's Pogo cards. Look, he's even got the whole collection. Isn't that cool?" Yasmin turned to give the folder to Omar and for the first time, saw the look on his face.

Complete.

Utter.

Embarrassment.

In a chorus of cackles, Harrison, Jason and Hannah

pointed at Omar, tears in their eyes.

"Yeah that collection might have been cool . . . in Year One," Harrison guffawed.

"We knew you liked *baby* things." Hannah was wiping tears from her eyes. "That's so cringe!"

Yasmin felt furious. At herself just as much as the kids who were teasing Omar.

"Leave him alone!" she tried to shout, but her voice died away in her throat. She looked to Ezra for support.

"Yeah, stop being mean. They're not babyish, they're just cards. I think it's cool!" Ezra stood in front of Omar, as if he could stop the kids' taunting laughter from reaching him that way.

But Jason stood up and beckoned for Harrison and Hannah to follow him. He had a mean edge to his voice as he looked Yasmin up and down and spat, "What do you know? You're just as big a baby as Omar. Look at you carrying a stuffed animal around. Aren't you supposed to be older than us?"

Jason took one last look at Levi. "*That's* just embarrassing."

Then the three kids gathered up their beach towels and bags and strode off down the seafront.

There was a horrible quiet, filled only with the sounds of seagulls squawking and waves crashing. It would have been peaceful if they hadn't just monumentally ruined their mission.

"Are . . . are you okay, Omar?" Jack asked quietly.

"Just go *away*," Omar shouted, staring at the ground.

Jack opened his mouth to speak but then shook his head and rushed off. Omar lifted his eyes and looked directly at Yasmin and Levi.

"You two. You say you're my guardians . . . but you have *ruined my life*. I'm going home. Right now." Omar turned on his heel, tossed his Pogo card folder to the ground and ran off to Tall Brother and Short Brother.

Yasmin felt Levi shuffle in her arms and suddenly,

the guilt balloon in her stomach BURST.

She dropped Levi, just as carelessly as Omar had dropped his Pogo cards.

"Whoa, watch it," Levi grunted as he hit the sand.

"You just *don't learn*, do you?" Yasmin fumed. "You say we're a team but you're always pulling these stupid pranks and embarrassing me!"

Ezra stepped forward and put a hand on Yasmin's shoulder. "Yas –"

"No. He's done this ever since coming into my life. He keeps embarrassing me and I'm sick of it now. *This* is exactly why you CAN'T COME TO YEAR 7 WITH US."

Ezra gasped and covered his hands with his mouth.

Yasmin thought the exploded guilt balloon would make her feel full, angry and hot. But instead she just felt . . . empty.

"We're sorry, Levi. We were going to tell you . . ." Ezra started to say, but Levi held a leg up.

"No need. I already knew," he sniffed.

Now it was Yasmin's turn to gasp. Levi knew this whole time?

"I heard you sayin' how much you don't want me around, behind my back! So I texted Mama Llama and told her to put me on my own solo mission." Levi's ears were twitching in agitation as he spoke.

"Since you know *everything,* Yasmin, you can finish this mission yerself! I'm out!"

Levi got up and started trotting away, across the hot sand.

"Wait, Levi!" Ezra shouted, but Levi wasn't turning back. "Yasmin, you've got to go after him, you can make it up. Don't leave it like this."

Yasmin didn't even acknowledge Ezra, instead watching the figure of Levi as it got smaller and smaller in the distance. I mean, he was pretty small to begin with so it didn't take long.

If Levi was going to be stubborn, then Yasmin would too. She'd do it even better than him.

"Come on," she finally said to Ezra. "Let's go home."

CHAPTER THIRTEEN
Kiss and Make Up

The atmosphere between Yasmin, Ezra and Omar following the spectacularly disastrous beach party could only be described as *awkwardddddddd*. He'd completely frozen them out from the moment they got back from the beach, all through their pizza dinner and right until the next morning. Auntie Rani suspected something was up and tried to get Yasmin to tell her, but Yasmin just shrugged and said everything was fine.

Everything was definitely not fine.

Not only was she failing her mission to help Omar, Levi had gone. She didn't know if she'd ever see him again.

It was another scorching day and since no one

felt like doing anything, Uncle Yusef filled up a paddling pool in the garden and turned the sprinklers on for the kids to play in. But Yasmin, Ezra and Omar just sat in the shade in silence, watching the sprinkler sway to and fro like a sad wave. If it wasn't one million degrees inside the house, Yasmin was sure her cousin would be holed up in his room, avoiding them.

"Well, this is just depressing," Ezra said finally. "And the sprinkler is wasting water if we aren't playing in it."

He jumped through it a few times but eventually sighed and turned it off at the taps. Turns out sprinklers weren't that much fun to play in alone.

"Can't you just apologise to Levi and get him to come back?" Ezra asked Yasmin, coming to sit on a lawn chair next to her.

"He should be apologising to me!" Yasmin pouted, feeling her body tense.

"You two are just as stubborn as each other," Ezra

said, shaking his head. "He might have been wrong about those stupid ideas at the beach, but we were wrong for not telling him the truth about Year 7. Sometimes you have to be the first one to apologise."

Yasmin listened to Ezra carefully – he could be very wise when he wanted to. As much as she tried to stay angry at Levi, the sadness she felt at him not being there was taking over. "Ugh, you're right, Ezra. But I can't apologise. He took the llama landline and I don't have any other way of contacting him. We should have just let him come to Year 7 with us . . . but it's too late now."

"I'm sorry, Yas." Ezra thought for a moment and then his face lit up. "Wait here, I've got an idea."

Yasmin watched as Ezra dashed back into the house and reappeared a short while later carrying coloured card, scissors and glue. Yasmin raised an eyebrow, wondering what on earth her friend was planning.

"I thought we could make Levi a little school tie in

the Riverbourne Academy colours," Ezra explained, putting the arts and crafts materials down in front of Yasmin. "That way, if he ever came back in the future, he'd be ready to join us in Year 7. Go on, Yassy, you're the arty one."

Yasmin chewed her lip. "That's nice, Ezra . . . but I don't know . . ."

Ezra was looking at her with such big, hopeful eyes that Yasmin didn't want to let him down. So she got stuck in, cutting strips of blue paper to stick over the green card in the shape of a tie. It felt good to be creative again and Yasmin remembered why she loved art in the first place. It made her feel calm inside.

When she was finished, Yasmin held up the tiny card tie with a loop of string attached and Ezra clapped.

"Thanks for thinking of this, Ezra, and thank you for the advice. You're the best best friend ever." Yasmin tried to smile, but it faded quickly. "But I have to be honest. I don't think Levi's coming back."

Ezra sighed. "I know . . . What are we going to do about the mission?"

They looked over at Omar, who was sitting on the other side of the garden, reading a book with a miserable look on his face.

(Which you aren't allowed to do with this book by the way, readers, big smiles only, *please*.)

Yasmin took a deep breath and tucked away the paper tie in a plastic wallet to keep it safe. Then she got to her feet with a determined energy.

"I'm going to finish the mission with Omar myself," she told Ezra.

"Okay, what's the plan?" her best friend asked.

"What we should have done from the start. Being honest."

Yasmin and Ezra approached Omar and sat down in front of him on the grass. He didn't look up from his book but his frown deepened.

"Omar, I know you hate me right now but I want to apologise. We never should have set up that party and not asked you first. Levi gets carried away sometimes and . . . well, he's gone now." Yasmin picked at the grass in front of her. "I do really want to help you though, that's true. Ezra does too."

"I do!" Ezra chipped in.

"Because I know what it feels like to be made fun of."

Omar's eyebrows twitched and he looked up from his book a little bit.

"You probably don't remember this, but I never used to speak," Yasmin continued.

"I remember," Omar said quietly.

Yasmin felt a little spark of hope light within her

and she pushed on. "Well, that didn't exactly make me friends at school. People used to think I was weird. To be honest, they still do. The friends I used to have stopped hanging out with me. Then when I started speaking, I got called Trombone by my brothers! I got made fun of either way."

"So how come it doesn't bother you?" Omar put his book down and looked at Yasmin with big brown eyes.

"Because I have friends . . . Levi helped me make friends." Yasmin felt her throat choke up and she swallowed it down. "It took a while but I trusted that Levi wanted to help me. Once I trusted him and Ezra, I didn't mind so much that other people teased me. Because I had a team."

Omar thought about this for a while and Yasmin felt Ezra pat her hand. She looked at him and saw he was smiling like he was proud of her.

"Those kids at the beach, Harrison, Hannah and Jason, they always pick on me," Omar said finally.

"At first they said I was babyish because they saw a Pogo card in my bag, but then it was for everything. They said my monkey pencil case was childish, they thought I was a wimp for holding my mum's hand in the playground . . . The teachers told them off but it didn't stop them. I got sick of it so I just started being mean back."

Ezra nodded. "I understand. But even if people are rude to you, you shouldn't be mean. Like Jack, he does actually want to be your friend."

"I do like Jack . . . I think I was scared he would tease me like the others." Omar chewed his lip. "But I was rude to him. Do you think he'd still want to be friends with me?"

Yasmin brightened. "Absolutely. You just need to tell him what you told us. Honesty is the best policy! But as for those *bullies* -"

"I don't want to be friends with them!" Omar said quickly. "Please don't talk to them. It could make things worse!"

Yasmin had to fight the urge to run out of the garden and hunt down every kid who had made fun of her younger cousin. Her family loyalty was kicking in. But she knew a guardian llama should act, not *react*.

"You don't have to talk to those kids. But you should definitely give Jack a chance. Having someone on your side makes everything better."

Yasmin's heart sank as she spoke. Levi was always on her side. But she'd let her embarrassment and the taunts of others get in the way of her friendship. Would she ever be able to apologise to him? He could be halfway to Peru by now . . .

"YASMINYOURBROTHERSAREGOINGTO THEARCADE," Ammi bellowed from inside the house.

"Why don't you all go with them?" Auntie Rani suggested, popping her head out of the patio door. "I'll give you some coins for the arcade games."

"That's where the kids from school hang out

sometimes." Omar seemed worried. But Yasmin squeezed his hand.

"We don't have to talk to the bullies. But Jack might be there. You can apologise to him and try to make friends?" She smiled hopefully.

"We won't leave your side the whole time," Ezra added. "And we won't make you do anything you don't want to either. This time."

Omar looked at Ezra and Yasmin with something they hadn't seen this whole holiday – a smile. It was small, true, and his eyes were kind of screwed up and squinting from the sun, but he was *definitely* smiling. Yasmin felt a warm, fuzzy feeling inside. Being honest meant Omar had opened up too. If only Levi was here to see it.

"Let's go," Omar said, nodding his head. "I'll try."

Ezra whooped, running and jumping into the paddling pool in celebration.

"Oops, can I get changed first?" he said, looking down at his wet swimming trunks.

Yasmin laughed and pulled Omar up from the grass with her. They were going to the arcade, they would help Omar make friends with Jack and maybe, *hopefully*, complete the mission.

Even if they had to do it without Levi.

CHAPTER FOURTEEN
Arcade Showdown

The arcade on Whitehove pier prided itself on being the third largest outdoor arcade in the UK. What they didn't mention was that there were only four outdoor arcades in the UK. In a country where it rained so much, having electrical equipment outdoors wasn't exactly the best business plan.

But there wasn't a drop of rain in sight as Yasmin, Ezra, Omar and Yasmin's brothers walked on to the huge wooden pier that jutted into the sea. The heatwave they were having meant the beach was busier than usual and most people were in the sea rather than playing the games. Yasmin was glad she'd brought a sun hat with her, and Ezra had put on a lot of sun cream before they left. Some of it was still sitting in a white blob on his nose, but Yasmin didn't say anything since it was making Omar giggle. She liked seeing her cousin happy for a change.

"Are you sure this is a good idea?" Omar said as they walked down the long pier towards the end where the games were.

"Definitely," Ezra replied. "You can apologise to Jack and then just have fun! I'm sure he still wants to be friends."

But as they approached the big archway that marked the start of the arcade, Yasmin knew why Omar was worried.

Harrison, Jason and Hannah were at the candyfloss stand buying sweets when they walked in. There was an awkward silence when the two groups clocked each other. Yasmin felt Omar shuffle closer towards her and she instantly stood a little taller, wanting to protect him.

"Right, losers, we're going to play Zombie Blast Xtreme," Tall Brother announced, breaking the silence.

"Yeah, here's your tokens." Short Brother dropped the coins into Yasmin's hand. But before he left he whispered into her ear, "Any problems, come get us."

Yasmin blinked at her brothers as they walked off, completely bemused. Had they actually offered to *help* her? They must have overheard the bullies at the beach the other day . . .

"Look, Jack's over there." Ezra nudged Omar, pointing to the Pac-Man game.

Yasmin was ready to launch into a pep talk, but to her surprise, Omar took a deep breath, puffed out his chest and strode on over to Jack. Yasmin and Ezra stayed a few steps behind to give them some space, but close enough to eavesdrop.

"Hi, Jack. I just wanted to say sorry for being mean to you the other day," Omar started, looking down at his feet.

"Oh, um. Thanks, Omar." Jack stopped his game and turned around.

"And sorry for the other times I've been rude. I think I just didn't believe you actually wanted to be friends with me . . ."

Jack cocked his head to one side. "Why would you think that? Of course I want to be friends with you. Actually . . . I want to apologise to *you*."

Omar's head popped up and he looked straight into Jack's eyes. "But why?"

"I should have stood up for you all those times when Hannah, Jack and Harrison were mean to you. But now that we're friends, we'll have each other's backs, right?" Jack smiled at Omar and his eyes sparkled.

"Right!" Omar replied, holding out his hand and the boys high-fived.

Yasmin felt a warmth spreading in her chest and realised she was beaming from ear to ear. She was proud of Omar! He was able to own up to his mistakes and apologise, and now he and Jack were friends. That took some serious bravery.

"I wish I could apologise to Levi . . ." Yasmin said quietly to Ezra. The sudden realisation that he wasn't there, sharing this moment, brought tears to her eyes. "We were supposed to have each other's backs too. But I cared too much about what other people would think."

"I know . . . I wish he was here. I never should have said he couldn't come to Year 7 with us. He's our friend." Ezra put his arm round Yasmin and they both retreated into their thoughts.

"Well, well, well. We should have known we'd find you over by the *baby* games," came a nasty voice from behind them.

Yasmin whirled round and saw Hannah, eating her candyfloss with a cruel smirk on her face.

"Yeah, Pac-Man is *so easy*," Harrison laughed.

Jason looked Yasmin up and down. "Where's your *teddy bear* today? Tucked up in bed with a blankie?"

"Leave us alone," said Ezra. "If you can't say something nice, then you shouldn't say anything at all."

But Yasmin's back had stiffened and her eyes narrowed. She'd *had it* with these kids. Even though Omar didn't want to confront them, she just couldn't let these bullies get away with being so mean.

"That's it!" she boomed in her low voice, catching everyone's attention. "I challenge you three to an arcade showdown. Whoever gets the most tickets wins. Then we'll see who's really the baby!"

"Yasmin, no, you don't have to do this!" Omar rushed forward, grabbing Yasmin's arm.

"Don't worry." Ezra held him back and whispered, "Yasmin's actually pretty sick at arcade games."

Harrison stepped forward. "Easy. You're on!"

Yasmin – 1 Bullies – 0

Next up, Yasmin takes on Jason at air hockey.

Yasmin – 1 Bullies – 1

Yasmin brings out the big guns. Yasmin – 2 Bullies – 1

With just one game left to go, Yasmin and the bullies are tied at 2 games each. Who will win?

CHAPTER FIFTEEN
Big Babies

It was down to the last game and whoever won would be the arcade champion. Yasmin needed to win. Her reputation and Omar's depended on it. Maybe if she could beat Harrison, Hannah and Jason in this showdown, they'd lay off Omar for a while.

It was Harrison's turn to choose a game and he pointed at a large, colourful and brightly lit machine in the middle of the arcade ground. The dance machine. Yasmin stepped forward to take up position but she felt a hand pull her back. It was Omar and he looked determined.

"No, Yasmin . . . No one's ever fought for me before. Seeing you go against them in all those games made me realise . . . I have to do this last battle alone." Omar looked seriously at Yasmin with his round baby face and she knew he was right.

"Okay, Omar. But remember, it doesn't matter who wins or loses. You're brave for just trying." Yasmin patted him on the back as he took his place on the dance platform.

"Yeah, yeah, that's what losers always say," Harrison laughed, standing on the adjacent dance platform.

"You've got this, Omar!" Jack cheered.

They entered their coins and the machine spurred into action, the screen flashing neon lights. The loud, driving music started and then they were off! Omar moved his feet to the corresponding arrows on the floor as quickly as possible and was doing well to hit them all. But Harrison was just as good, stamping out the rhythms and getting high point scores. By their second round a small audience had gathered, consisting of some other kids that Jack said went to their school, and a few of their parents who watched the battle rage on.

It was the most intense dance battle Yasmin had ever witnessed. Even more intense than the series finale of *Are You the Greatest Dancer? UK*.

"Uhhh, Harrison?" Ezra tapped the boy's arm but he was too busy dancing to notice.

"Hey! He's trying to cheat and distract Harrison," Jason complained, pointing at Ezra.

"I'm not! I'm just trying to warn him . . . his jeans are falling down," Ezra said in a slightly quieter voice.

Yasmin's eyes bugged and she looked over to see Harrison's cool baggy jean shorts drooping down as he aggressively stomped to the beat. At this rate they'd be around his ankles by the end of the song!

Then a voice called out from the assembled crowd. "Hey, look! Harrison wears teddy bear pants! He's a big baby!"

Harrison's jean shorts had dropped down so far that

they revealed his baby-blue teddy-bear-print pants!

Everyone in the crowd burst out laughing and Harrison quickly scrambled to pull up his shorts, turning bright red. The game finished and Omar won, since Harrison had missed all the beats at the end of the game. But no one even noticed that

Omar had won. They were too busy pointing and laughing at Harrison.

Yasmin caught Ezra's eye and saw the crease between his eyebrows. This wasn't right. Even if Harrison was a bully, making fun of him wasn't the way to make things better. She had to do something. No, she had to *say* something.

"Everyone, stop!" she shouted, silencing the assembled crowd. "Why are you making fun of him for having 'childish' underwear? Aren't we all still children? Why can't we like childish things? Being a child is much more fun than being an adult."

"That's true," said one man, standing watching with his son.

"We all like different things and we all have our 'weird' hobbies. Everyone's different. That's what makes us unique." Yasmin dug deep and spoke from her heart. "I used to think I was weird. I thought I should just be quiet and try to blend in with everyone else. But then I found friends who made me realise that the things that make me 'weird' make me *special*."

Ezra smiled at Yasmin and shouted, "I still sleep with my blankie! I love being weird!"

A few people in the crowd laughed and then a small girl with pigtails shouted, "I have tea parties with my cat. I love being weird too!"

Yasmin watched as, one by one, everyone in the crowd started piping up.

"I always make a wish when an eyelash falls out," said a woman, holding a baby in her arms. "Some people think it's childish, but it makes me happy."

"I get my mum to check under the bed for monsters every night," said a tall boy.

Yasmin couldn't believe it. Sharing her 'weirdness' was encouraging everyone around them to do the same. She glanced over at Omar who seemed just as surprised as her. It turned out everyone had things that might seem childish or weird, but no one was embarrassed of them any more!

"I wear goggles in the bath," Hannah said quietly,

though she smiled a bit. "I like to pretend I'm scuba diving."

"That's so weird," Jason laughed. "...I do that too!"

Omar came forward and held Yasmin's hand. Then he shouted, "I like Pogo cards and my monkey pencil case!"

Yasmin felt that warm, proud feeling again and she lifted her head upwards. She closed her eyes and shouted, "I love my toy llama Levi and I don't

care who knows it. I wish he was here!"

At that moment, with her eyes still closed, she heard cackling above her. A harsh, annoying laugh she knew too well. She opened her eyes and there, riding across the blue sky on a massive seagull . . . was Levi!

"Ha ha!" he laughed, poking his tongue out. "You said you love me!"

"Levi!" shouted Yasmin, Levi and Omar in unison.

The seagull swooped down on to the candyfloss stand's roof and let Levi off. Levi slipped him a couple of chips as payment before scaling down the back pole of the stand. Yasmin, Ezra and Omar rushed over, leaving everyone still confessing their weird and wonderful quirks to each other.

Yasmin dropped to her knees and Levi hopped up into her arms.

"Levi, I'm so sorry!" she gushed,

"No, I'm sorry –" Levi cut in.

"All right, all right, one at a time," Ezra laughed. "But also . . . I'm sorry."

Yasmin looked Levi in his beady eyes and felt a massive rush of relief that he was back.

"I should never have felt embarrassed to take you to Year 7. I thought people would make fun of me, but now I realise it doesn't matter what other people say. You're my best friend. That means accepting you for who you are. Which is a loud, wacky talking llama."

Levi wiped a single tear from his eye. "That was beautiful, Yassy. But I've been a fur-brained idiot too. I shouldn't have pulled those surprises without asking ya first. And I shouldn't have left just like that. You're my partner."

Then Levi looked over at Omar, who was standing awkwardly behind Ezra. "I saw you take on that dance battle. That was well brave, mate."

Omar smirked, "Thanks. So . . . you're actually, like, really . . . magic?"

Levi did a backflip in Yasmin's hands. "Sure am."

"I mean, I did see you fly in on a seagull. My friend's robot dog can't do *that*," Omar laughed.

Yasmin suddenly worried that Levi's aerial entrance might have drawn attention, but when she looked back over to the dance mats, the crowd had dispersed and Hannah, Jason, Harrison and Jack were chatting to each other.

I guess everyone was too busy confessing to notice the flying llama, she thought.

Yasmin held Levi out, as they went back over to the dance mats, no longer keeping him hidden away in a bag. Harrison had turned back to a normal colour now and his jean shorts were firmly pulled up to his waist. Omar walked right up to the group, holding his head high.

"So I guess we're all big babies then?" he said, looking to Harrison, Jason and Hannah.

"I guess so." Jason shrugged.

"You know, you made me feel really bad when you teased me," Omar continued. "Now you know how it feels. I hope you won't make fun of me or anyone else again."

Levi whistled, though of course, only Yasmin, Ezra and Omar could hear it. "Go on, my son!"

"We're sorry. We shouldn't have made fun of you," Harrison said first, shuffling his feet.

"We won't do it any more," Hannah added. "You know, I actually collect Pogo cards too. But I didn't tell anyone because I was afraid of being made fun of. Now you've made me feel braver to bring them to school again."

"Good. Pogo cards are awesome." Omar smiled.

The three former bullies left, leaving Yasmin, Ezra, Omar, Jack and Levi by the now empty dance mats. There was a beeping noise and Yasmin saw Levi flip open the llama landline. He smiled at the screen and then turned it around for Yasmin to see.

Message received at 16.30
From: MAMA LLAMA

To: Agent Yasmin and Agent Levi

MISSION COMPLETE

CONGRATULATIONS AGENTS!

Yasmin raised her fist to the air and cheered. Then she eyed up the dance machine.

"Anyone for another round?"

CHAPTER SIXTEEN
It's a Miracle!

The Omar that came back through the door at Auntie Rani's house that afternoon was not the same boy that left. Well, I mean, technically it was, but in terms of his attitude, he was *completely* different. When they got in from the pier it was late afternoon and Yasmin's brothers both went upstairs to have a 'siesta' (they were becoming really lazy teenagers). Auntie Rani was sitting with Ammi and Papa in the open-plan living room and kitchen when they got back, a fan blowing full blast on their bodies. The first thing Omar did when they stepped through the door was give his mum a hug.

"Hi, Mum, missed you," he said, then walked into the kitchen. "Can I have a snack?"

Auntie Rani was so overjoyed that Yasmin thought she might start jumping up and down. "Yes, my *jaan*. Any snacks you'd like! I can make samosas? Or chapli kebabs?"

She rushed into the kitchen and started whipping out pots and pans, cooking in a joy-frenzy.

"I'll have one of each," Levi said in Yasmin's arms, making Omar giggle.

"I'm going to go say hi to Dad too." Omar smiled, stopping by Ammi and Papa sitting in the living room on his way upstairs. "I'm glad you came to visit, Khalajee. You too, Khalujee."

Papa blinked in surprise and Ammi held her hands together in a prayer position.

"Alhamdullilah," she whispered. "NOWGOSEE YOURPAPA."

Omar laughed at Ammi's loudness and bounded up the stairs.

Yasmin was a bit surprised at how dramatic the adults were being over Omar's new happy mood, but then she realised they must have been very worried about him.

"Yasmin, Ezra, what did you do?" Auntie Rani beamed, her eyes shining. "He's like my old Omar again."

Ezra looked to Yasmin and she stepped forward, letting him know she was okay to explain.

"We found out that Omar was having some problems with a group of kids in his class. But we spoke to them and it won't be an issue any more. Plus, we helped him make a new friend, Jack."

Auntie Rani shook her head. "Oh my gosh, I knew something was happening at school, but he just wouldn't speak to us!"

"He just needed two guardian llamas to open up to!" Levi said, poking Yasmin in the ribs. She suppressed a giggle.

"Don't worry," Ezra added. "They won't be teasing him any more. If they do, Jack will have his back."

"We must have this Jack around for tea!" Auntie

Rani clapped her hands together, seeming much brighter "Oh, I'm just so relieved. It's a miracle!"

She grabbed Yasmin and Ezra, hugging them tightly and squishing Levi in the process.

"It's not a miracle, it was hard work actually, lady!" Levi complained, getting thoroughly squashed.

But Yasmin was happy her auntie didn't have to worry any more. Now there was another matter to attend to.

Yasmin and Ezra dashed upstairs to Omar's room, making Levi wait outside the door whilst they got ready. Then they called out, "Okay, come in!"

"This better be good!" Levi said, swaggering in and hopping up on the chest of drawers. "I'm expecting a song and dance . . . or at least a cake."

Yasmin cleared her throat. "Just listen, furball! We're trying to apologise."

"I'm all ears." Levi winked and sat himself down.

"So, Levi. Like we said before, we're so sorry for saying we don't want you to come to Year 7 with us," Yasmin began.

"So sorry," Ezra confirmed.

"Like I said on the pier, you're my best friend and I accept all your weirdness, just like you accept mine," Yasmin continued.

"And you do have *a lot* of weirdness," Levi winked.

"Anyway . . . what I'm trying to say is -" Yasmin held the little tie she'd made out of card in front of her, making sure the Riverbourne Academy colours were on full display.

"Will you come to Year 7 with us?" Yasmin and Ezra shouted together.

Levi's beady eyes went the biggest Yasmin had ever seen them, and she swore she could even see a little blush in his cheeks.

"Oh, you two . . . thank you!" he said, letting Yasmin put the little tie around his neck. "But no."

Yasmin's mouth dropped open. "WHAT?"

"Yeah . . . naaa. I don't really want to," Levi laughed. "No offence, but when I really thought about it, travelling the world seems much more exciting than going to secondary school."

"But, but . . . we're a team!" Yasmin was flabbergasted. After all that trouble they had had over not wanting Levi to come, and now *he* didn't even want to go to Year 7 any more!

"Listen, Yassy, watching you complete the mission with Omar alone . . . I knew you didn't need me any more," Levi said gently. "And I don't need you either. We've learned a lot from each other, but on solo missions we can help twice as many people. Even if we aren't guardian llama partners, we'll still be best friends."

Yasmin felt the initial shock melt away and then she started giggling. A little bit at first but then more and more, until she was properly belly laughing.

"Why are we laughing?" Ezra said, chuckling along too.

"Yasmin's finally lost it!" Levi laughed along.

Yasmin picked him up and hugged him tight. "I just realised I'm so sad that I'm losing my guardian llama partner and . . . It's just so *weird*."

"It is weird, isn't it?" Levi hugged her back. "Are you okay with going solo though, Yassy?"

Yasmin nodded. "More than okay. Plus, I've got the best bodyguard ever."

Ezra cheered. "Yes! Bodyguard status confirmed!"

Levi hopped out of Yasmin's arms and landed on the bed, holding one leg aloft.

"Right then, the mission is complete, so that means there's only one thing left to do –

"Have the best holiday ever!"

Time to say goodbye.

Yasmin hugged her little cousin tightly as they said goodbye. The last few days they'd had on holiday had really been the best ever and she felt so lucky to have spent it with not only her best friends but her family too.

"Thank you, Yasmin," Omar said quietly. "You're the best guardian llama *and* cousin ever."

Yasmin smiled back. "You're welcome. And don't worry, I've already asked Ammi and we can come back next year."

"Bye, kid, good luck," Levi said, perched on Yasmin's shoulder.

"I wish I wasn't going to forget you," Omar said sadly. Yasmin had warned Omar this would happen since the mission had ended and she felt it was best to warn him. Luckily, a quick text to Mama Llama meant they were able to put it off until the holiday had ended.

"Ah, I'm sure there'll be plenty more annoying people in your life," Levi winked. "Every time someone irritates you, you'll remember me somewhere in your heart . . ."

Omar chuckled and wiped a little tear from his eye. Next, he gave Ezra a big hug and asked him to come back next year too.

It was an emotional goodbye, but Ammi was ready to get on the road.

As they pulled away, Yasmin saw Auntie Rani, Uncle Yusef and Omar standing smiling together and she knew her mission was complete.

CHAPTER SEVENTEEN
Once a Cockney
Geezer . . .

The car ride home from Whitehove was just as chaotic as the one going there. Not even a week's holiday could calm Ammi's road rage. But Yasmin managed to nap most of the way home. She was finding it much easier to relax since she'd got rid of the guilt balloon in her stomach. It was like Levi always said after a burp – "Better out than in."

They arrived back to number 11 Fish Lane very late at night, thanks to a lot of traffic on the motorway, and everyone was exhausted. Papa had called Ezra's mum to say he could stay at their house that night since it was so late and Levi was fast asleep in Yasmin's arms. If he wasn't so grubby, Yasmin might have even gone so far as to say he looked cute. As they all trooped in the front door, Yasmin was surprised to see Auntie Bibi and Auntie Gigi sitting at the kitchen table, cups of chai in hand.

"So how was the holiday?" Auntie Bibi began.

"Yes, tell us everything!" Auntie Gigi enthused.

"Agh, sisters. Tomorrow," Papa groaned, rubbing his eyes.

"WEAREEXHAUSTED," Ammi yawned/shouted, already lugging her suitcase up the stairs.

Yasmin's aunties were *not pleased,* and sighed dramatically.

"Humph, this is the welcome we get?" Auntie Gigi frowned. "Anyway, Yasmin, there is a letter here for you."

"Yes, we've been waiting all week to see what it says." Auntie Bibi wiggled her eyebrows and slid a letter towards Yasmin on the table. Yasmin knew her aunties would have tried to peek inside to see what it said. They loved being the first to know things.

Everyone watched Yasmin open the letter. Even Ammi waited on the stairs to see.

Yasmin took a deep breath and read it aloud:

Fish Lane Primary School
Brick Lane
London

Dear Yasmin,

It has been an absolute pleasure teaching you this term and seeing you blossom into a caring and responsible student. You and Ezra have done brilliantly supporting other students throughout the school and it hasn't gone unnoticed by us teachers.

That is why I am happy to tell you that we have nominated you and Ezra as joint Head Prefects for Year 7 when you join Riverbourne Academy! You will be the spokespeople for your year group and support everyone as they get used to the new school. The headteacher there is looking forward to meeting you and telling you more about the role, but you should be very proud of yourselves.

I will be writing to Ezra separately to inform him of the good news as well.

Looking forward to seeing you for our final term together.

Best wishes,

Miss Zainab

There was a huge cheer in the kitchen that woke Levi up from his slumber.

"What? What are we celebrating?" he stammered with bleary eyes.

"Me and Yasmin are Head Prefects for Year 7!" Ezra gasped, looking at Yasmin with wide eyes.

They gave each other a big hug and Yasmin felt her ammi and papa join in too.

"HEADPREFECT!" Ammi beamed.

"We couldn't be prouder, Yasmin!" Papa said, squeezing them tight.

Yasmin felt a huge smile stretch across her face. She was proud too.

Later when they were up in her bedroom, Yasmin read the letter again so Levi could hear what it said.

"Head Prefect, woo," Levi whistled. "I guess a guardian llama's work is never done! Speaking of which . . ."

Yasmin and Ezra watched as Levi jumped down off the bed and scrambled underneath. They heard him rummaging around under there for a while before he emerged, carrying a black cardboard box.

"You really need to clean under your bed Yassy, it's gross." He wrinkled his nose.

"Whatever!" Yasmin laughed. "What is that?"

Levi held the box out to her and she took it, opening the top carefully. Inside was a shiny silver flip phone, with the logo 'LL' embossed on the top.

"A llama landline!" Yasmin gasped, taking the phone out.

"I was gonna give it to ya on your first day of Year 7," Levi explained. "But now we can use it to stay in touch when I'm away on missions. Your very own llama landline. You earned it!"

Yasmin grabbed Levi and gave him a kiss right on his grubby nose.

"Ew!" he laughed, wiping it off. "I take it you like the pressie then?"

"I love it!" Yasmin passed the phone to Ezra so he could have a look. But Ezra's eyes were watering.

"I . . . I'm gonna miss you, Levi." Ezra's lip trembled as he tried to hold back the tears.

Seeing Ezra cry made Yasmin's eyes well up too!

"Oh, stop it, you two, you'll set me off!" Levi waved a leg in front of his face. "Don't worry, I'll be back all the time. Whitechapel's me home. Once a cockney geezer, *always* a cockney geezer."

Yasmin nodded sadly and wiped her eyes. She couldn't imagine life without Levi's annoying but funny little voice always piping up at the wrong times. Without watching TV with biscuits on a Friday night with him, or hearing him snore at the end of the bed. Her rucksack would always feel a bit empty without him hiding inside it when she was out and about.

But then, a year ago, Yasmin wouldn't have been able to imagine a life where she spoke out loud, communicated with her parents and had a best friend like Ezra. Things were always changing and they were so often for the better.

"So this is our last ever sleepover together?" Yasmin said, looking at Ezra and Levi sitting on her bed.

Levi nodded. "I gotta head to the London paddock tomorrow and then they'll transport me to Peru for my next mission."

"In that case . . . we have to do every sleepover game ever. Pillow fights, truth or dare, midnight feasts – let's do it all!" Yasmin rubbed her hands together.

"Are you sure it isn't too 'babyish'?" Ezra teased.

Yasmin picked up a pillow and whacked Ezra with it. "No way!"

After all, being a child is *way* more exciting than being an adult.

CHAPTER EIGHTEEN
The End(s)

You did it, reader! You made it to the end of the book! How do you feel . . . older? Well, you are in fact older now than when you started reading. But who cares? Just like Yasmin and Ezra have proven, getting older doesn't mean the fun *or* the magic disappears. You might have to look harder for it, but it's there. Talking toy llamas are just one (very weird) example. But don't you just love being weird?

Yasmin and Ezra were standing in the big hallway of Riverbourne Academy in their second week of Year 7. They were waiting for the lunch bell to ring so they could help guide Year 7s to the cafeteria before the older kids came out of their classes and stampeded them. Yasmin still hadn't got used to the blazer, but she liked the big shiny 'Head Prefect' badge that was pinned to the lapel.

She and Ezra had taken to their Head Prefect duties very quickly. It turned out there was a lot of crossover between being a guardian llama and a Year 7 prefect. And even though Tall Brother and Short Brother had told Yasmin NEVER to talk to them in school, they also told her and Ezra to come find them if they ever had any problems with other kids. Yasmin knew she could look after herself in that respect, but it was nice of her brothers to offer.

The lunch bell rang and Year 7s started filtering out of their classrooms into the corridor.

"This way, please," Ezra was bellowing and Yasmin did her best hand waving to get the Year 7s into an orderly queue.

The llama landline buzzed in her pocket and, even though they technically weren't allowed phones at school, she picked it up.

"Hello? Is your refrigerator running?" a voice said on the other end of the line.

Yasmin rolled her eyes. "Levi! I know it's you! This is the third time this week!"

Levi cackled on the other end of the line, "Sorry, love. It's just still so funny."

Yasmin couldn't help but laugh too. "Look, I have to go, I'm on duty!"

"All right, all right. Me too. But catch up later?"

"Defo." Yasmin smiled. "Bye!"

"Ta-ra!" Levi said, before hanging up the phone.

All the students were coming out for lunch now and the corridor was heaving with students. One small boy with a huge rucksack hurried past Yasmin and Ezra, muttering something under his breath. Yasmin looked closer and spotted a small white llama head poking out of his bag.

"Don't worry, everything's going to be fine," the llama was saying to the boy as they passed by.

Yasmin and Ezra caught each other's eye and giggled.

"Well . . ." Yasmin shrugged. "You're never too old for a guardian llama."

Acknowledgements

The journey of Levi and Yasmin has been a long one. In 2017, I won a scholarship to the Winchester Writers' Festival, where I was able to meet three agents to pitch them ideas. In the long list of people to thank, I'd firstly like to say a big thank you to Judith Heneghan and the panel who awarded me that scholarship.

I met my wonderful agent Davinia Andrew-Lynch at that festival and showed her the first three chapters of *Llama Out Loud*. I was shocked that it wasn't actually complete rubbish and that my weird story about a talking toy llama might even be funny! She encouraged me to write the rest and helped me with countless drafts. So I really cannot thank you enough, Davinia, for everything! This simply would not have happened without you.

I would also like to thank Allen Fatimaharan for

his amazing contributions to this series. His talent and humour have elevated each book more than I could have imagined. I hope we get to work together again.

Of course, I want to say a big thank you to everyone at Farshore for giving Levi and Yasmin a home! Special thanks to my editor Liz Bankes, Asmaa Isse and Aleena Hasan. Thanks also to the design team for making the books look so eye-catching and fun!

Writing these books has been everything from ridiculous fun to the hardest I've ever worked, but I'm so proud of them and the joy they've brought to readers. Having the series debut in the middle of a pandemic was heartbreaking to say the least, so a thank you to my friends who were there for me through the hard times – Helena, you are the best.

My sister Chloe and my parents Naveed and Lisa, I get all my funniest stories from you! I love you all so much. Thank you, Mama, for always taking us to bookshops as children and teaching us that books are magical. I'm a writer because of you.

Finally, thank you to my partner Betty, who always celebrates me and reminds me that I am, in fact, good enough. Love you forever.

Check out book 1!

Check out book 2!

'Anarchically silly fun' *Guardian* on *Llama Out Loud*

LLAMA ON A MISSION

ILLUSTRATED BY ALLEN FATIMAHARAN

ANNABELLE SAMI